MOSTLY TRUE

Short Stories

Arlene N. Cohen

Mostly True
Short Stories

ISBN 978-0-9986877-8-0

A catalog record for this book is available from the Library of Congress

Dedication

To my Friends and Family

Other Books by Arlene

Stories on the Move: Integrating Literature and
Movement with Children from Infant to Age 14 (2007)
Published by Libraries Unlimited/ABC-CLIO

Forthcoming 2020

Literacy on the Move Series:
The Dancing Chameleons (for ages 2-6)
The Dancing Reptiles (for ages 4-8)
The Dancing Dogs (for ages 6-10)

The Dancing Chameleons Coloring and Activity Book
The Dancing Reptiles Coloring and Activity Book
The Dancing Dogs Coloring and Activity Book

Contents

Introduction:
What's it all about, anyway?

Let's be honest; admit it: "Most of what we set out to do never meets our expectations." This concept may not satisfy the perfectionist; but, then what does? People never make mistakes… intentionally. An honest mistake is as good as no mistake at all, right? No one intends to blunder. In youth, we blame our errors on 'lack of experience'. As senior citizens, we package our bloopers as 'senior moments'. In between times, we call it 'fate'.

But…creating causes just diffuses reality and how we handle what actually happens. Life is what it is and things are just what they are; why label them? The journey can't be codified. It's a bumpy trek!

Of course, we have choices when we encounter a conflict: we can give up, run away, push through, pray, or even change our perspective; for relief, we can laugh at this 'comedy of errors'. If you see yourself in any of these scenarios, please have a few laughs on me.

The Livin' Doll

"Acting is behaving truthfully under imaginary circumstances."
~ Sanford Meisner, Actor and Acting Instructor

"Children see magic because they look for it."
~Christopher Moore, Author

Five-year old Roslyn doesn't spend time playing with plastic dollies. She doesn't need to; a real live doll lives just down the street, in a richly decorated dollhouse. Roslyn enjoys playing a movie game with her Livin' Doll almost every day. After breakfast, Roslyn puts her shiny brown hair in a ponytail and dashes off for a bit of Hollywood glamour with her doll. The Livin' Doll is a feisty 60ish retired actress named Pauline. At age five, Roslyn enjoys repetition and, most of all, learning what it takes to be a star. As for Pauline, she welcomes the daily encore.

"Oh, good morning, Dah...ling, do come in," the diminutive Pauline says in a raspy, dramatic voice, as she opens the heavy dark wood door of her dollhouse. She sounds a bit like Greta Garbo, an actress from the era of her performance career. Pauline hasn't donned her costume yet; she is still in her nightgown and flowing, richly-patterned silk robe from the orient.

The doll's piano is covered in a fringed gold and maroon brocade coverlet. The same rich fabric drapes the windows, blocking outside light. One can barely see the maroon velvet upholstered furnishings in the glow of the crystal chandelier, but there is no missing the intricately designed blue and red Persian carpet spread across the walnut floors. Roslyn is stepping onto a replica of a silent movie set from the 20's.

Pauline loves birds. She has a red, green, yellow, and blue parrot named "Anna." For most of the performance, Anna is hidden under a cloth that covers her bird cage, in the bedroom. Pauline's bleached-blond hair is a mess when she first gets up. She has a lot of hair. Roslyn loves Anna and wonders if Pauline ever lets the bird roost in her hair, which in many ways resembles a nest until she has performed her coiffure routine.

"Are you ready to begin, Rosie?" This is Roslyn's cue.

"The performance must go on, Pauline," Roslyn remarks.

Pauline points toward her boudoir. "Enter stage left, dear, and take a front row seat." Roslyn enters Pauline's bedroom, folding the skirt of her blue striped dress under her as she sits down on a pink velvet chair, near the closet. She recites her lines from there.

The first scene has begun, called "The Actress Chooses her Costume". In her trailing silk robe, Pauline poses and ponders by her wardrobe closet, looking over her outfits. Pauline's costumes are custom-made by a Hollywood dressmaker, all from the same pattern, just like sets of doll clothes, which have been crayoned in an array of colors. Pauline's selection consists entirely of matching the color with her mood; it is that simple. Today is a turquoise day.

"Let's see, what shall I wear today? This one is flattering, wouldn't you say, Rosie?" Pauline pulls out her costume, a turquoise gabardine suit and a white nylon blouse. It is Roslyn's second cue.

She answers in her excited little voice, "Oh, yes, that one is perfect." She knows and says her lines well. Pauline bows to Roslyn who giggles and applauds.

"I wore turquoise on the set in 'Return to Me'; it was my very first movie, filmed on location in Hawaii, Rosie."

"Hawaii? Where is that?"

"It is across a big ocean, called the Pacific. That is where I was."

"Oh, a big ocean! You went across a big ocean?"

"Yes and in the movie, I swam in the turquoise-colored sea with dolphins. I was the Esther Williams of the sea, doing my ballet in the waves. Crowds gathered on the set to watch my performance. You may not have seen it; it was a several years ago. I was beautiful. I was graceful. I was stunning."

They laugh as Pauline goes into the wardrobe closet to change into her outfit. When Pauline opens the closet door, Roslyn stands up and together they recite 3 phrases and take 3 poses: "I am beautiful. I am graceful. I am stunning." They repeat the phrases and poses 3 more times, more dramatically each time.

Sitting down, Roslyn recites her third line: "Oh, I can see you, Pauline, so beautiful, so sparkling."

"Oh, thank you dah...ling; you always say the sweetest things. Those were the days. Now I must choose my footwear."

Scene 2 has begun: "The Actress Chooses her Shoes". Roslyn looks down as Pauline selects a pair of turquoise socks and shoes. Her shoes are also custom-made by a Hollywood shoemaker and she has them in the same colors as the suits. Except for the color, they look exactly alike, fluted, opened-toed wedges with shoelaces. Seated, Pauline places them on her small feet and ties them carefully. She raises her leg and turns her foot back and forth to show off her gorgeous footwear. This is Roslyn's next cue.

Loudly, Roslyn shouts as Pauline has taught her, "Beautiful! Your feet are beautiful, Pauline!"

"Shush, Sweetie, not that loud; you might wake Saulie and Anna." Saulie is Pauline's husband, who lives in the room next door. In his plaid shirts and khakis and suspenders, he looks like 'Old MacDonald', the farmer in Roslyn's storybook. He doesn't have many lines, except for a few later in the performance.

Scene 3 has begun: "The Actress Puts on Her Makeup." Without further ado, Pauline slides gracefully onto the violet velvet bench of her antique vanity that has three gold-embossed drawers on each side and a huge etched oval mirror in the center. In this scene, Pauline opens the ornate drawers and pulls out her bejeweled makeup kits. Roslyn doesn't wear makeup yet, but she hopes one day that she will make herself beautiful just like Pauline. She doesn't want to miss any of the steps, so she moves her chair close to the vanity and watches closely.

Quite out of the ordinary set of events, Pauline stops everything right there and stares at her image in the mirror nervously picking at her bird's nest of hair, saying, "I just did it last week."

"What did you do last week, Pauline?" Roslyn asks, startled by the break in the routine.

"Oh, nothing...nothing; never mind."

Roslyn is astonished by her sharp tone. *Pauline never said or talked like that before.* Pauline keeps picking at her bird's nest hair. *Maybe Anna laid an egg in there.* Thinking that makes Roslyn giggle.

Pauline turns and glares at Roslyn. "What's so funny?"

"Oh, nothing. Really. I'm sorry." Roslyn answers quickly.

"All right, we must now get on with the performance!" Pauline announces.

Roslyn smiles.

As Pauline dabs and re-dabs her face with a light pinkish powder, Roslyn dabs her face and lifts her chin, just like Pauline. Next, when Pauline curls her eyelashes with a scissors-like thing and paints her lashes with black mascara, Roslyn mimics her movements. Using a single bold stroke of a colored pencil, Pauline draws her eyebrow lines with her chin tilted upwards. Roslyn sweeps her finger over her eyebrows with her chin angled up. Last but not least, Pauline carefully presses a tube of bright red lipstick upon and beyond her lips, making them look youthfully full. This is Roslyn's next cue.

"Oh, Pauline; you shine!"

"That comes next, dear. Pay attention."

"Oh, I'm sorry, Pauline."

Pauline stops again to glare at her hair in the mirror and shifts the ratted topknot back and forth, side to side. Roslyn is sure some bird seed will topple out at any minute; but it doesn't.

Scene 4 has begun: "The Actress Selects Her Jewelry". "Now it is time for adornment." From her velvet red heart-shaped jewelry box, Pauline draws out some flashy rhinestone earrings, and a matching necklace, ring, and bracelet.

"One must select the appropriate accessories, Rosie. Always choose those that catch the eye and keep it there. One must never forsake one's presence."

Roslyn doesn't quite know what 'forsake one's presence' means; but, she really likes the sparkling jewelry.

"Now dear, now you say it…shine…shine."

"Oh, Pauline, you shine. You twinkle."

Pauline gets up and joins hands with Roslyn and they dance in a circle, singing, "A twinkle here, a twinkle there… that is what makes a star."

Again, Pauline, seeing her reflection in the mirror, is distracted by her hair which has loosened more and now exposes the gray roots that are peeking through. "Oh, no!" Her eyes bulge, as she edges closer to the glass. How can this be? I just…"

"You just what?" Roslyn asks.

"Nothing; it's really nothing."

"How could I have missed those?" She touches the dark roots of her hair.

These lines aren't familiar; Roslyn is stumped.

"Saulie, Saulie, come right away." Pauline yells through the wall. Pauline brushes her hair furiously. "Saulie, oh Saulie," Pauline calls out in a shrill soprano voice, "Saulie, I need you N-O-W."

Anna, the parrot, wakes up and chimes in, "Saulie, Saulie, come right away, Saulie." Pauline pulls the cover off of the bird cage. The bird steps side-to-side and stretches her feathers.

"Hello, Rosie," says the bird.

"Good Morning, Anna," Roslyn says, leaving her seat to go scratch the bird's golden head.

Pauline's dutiful husband, wearing simple white long john underwear, wanders into the room, yawning.

"Saulie, I need some more lemons. I need you to go to the market and buy some lemons for my hair TODAY."

"More lemons, Saulie," says the bird.

"Yes, my love; I'll get you some at Alexander's Market this afternoon."

"Very good, Saulie; now, don't forget."

"I won't; I won't," said Saulie, as he yawns on his way out of the room.

"Don't forget, Saulie, more seeds, Saulie," squawks Anna, pushing the empty seed shells out the cup attached to the side of her cage.

"Yes, Anna," answers Saulie.

"Don't go back to sleep; go now!" Pauline yells.

"Don't go back to sleep; go now!" Anna shrieks.

"OK, OK." Saulie grumbles. "I'm on my way."

"Your line, Saulie; don't forget your line."

Saulie wanders back into the room. "Oh, good morning, Rosie. How is the young princess today?"

Roslyn giggles. "I'm fine, Saulie."

"She does fine; now, be on your way," Pauline says.

"Goodbye, Saulie." says Anna.

By the time Saulie leaves, Pauline has carefully rearranged her nest of hair to cover up the grey roots. Pauline, fully dressed, shoes, makeup, and jewelry leaves center stage and climbs onto her bed for her "Finale". She is a Livin' Doll beautifully poised on a shelf.

Roslyn looks with admiration at her gorgeous Livin' Doll. Pauline beams and turns her head side-to-side, as if she is being photographed. Pauline and Roslyn join hands and say, "The End." Roslyn claps and Anna chuckles and squawks.

"Someday, I am going to be a big movie star, just like you, Pauline!"

"That is for sure, Roslyn! You are very talented. Now, Sweetheart, I would like you to gather some new paperbacks from the neighborhood for me today. I need new romances, and mysteries are always good."

"I will do that, Pauline; I'll get you a lot of books. Can I still take Anna to school on a leash when I start kindergarten?"

Anna squawks and chuckles.

"Of course, dear."

The performance, a little different this time, is over; but, as always, Roslyn, one step closer to stardom, dances her way home, singing: "I am beautiful. I am graceful. I am stunning."

The Sixth Graders

"Only where children gather is there any real chance of fun."
~ Mignon McLaughlin, Journalist and Author

"No, I'm not going to listen to some silly story. That's for little kids. I'm twelve," said Keone, a husky Hawaiian-Samoan boy from Kalihi Elementary School. He spoke out so everyone in the classroom could hear him respond to the teacher. Ms. Chambers, a short slim Haole teacher from the Mainland, had just made the announcement that a storyteller would be coming next week to entertain them. Keone's buddies cheered him on and shook their fists and flexed their muscles and threw a few wads of paper at the girls in the front row. The girls turned around and made faces at them.

"Shut you face, Keone!" the three girls shouted in unison.

The other students moved restlessly in their seats and began chatting with the kids next to them. The whole class was out of order from the moment Keone opened his mouth.

Undaunted, Ms. Chambers clapped her hands loudly and tapped on her desk with a drumstick to get their attention. "Don't be so sure," she exclaimed. "This is a different kind of storyteller."

"Yeah, different how?" Keone inquired. Everyone wanted to know the answer to this question. She had their attention.

"She tells stories for older children and she dances the story."

"She gonna do one hula?" Ask Keone.

"I don't think so," responded Ms. Chambers

"What den? She gonna hip-hop?" asked Keone's best friend, Lyle. Lyle took the opportunity to demonstrate hopping left and right and then down on the floor doing a spin. Everyone clapped, and Lyle got up and gave a wave.

"Yo man, like that." Keone looked at Ms. Chambers and the rest of the class that was cheering like no tomorrow. Obviously, that might make the storyteller worth watching in their eyes. Ms. Chambers clapped again and struck her desk. "Possibly," she answered. "We will just have to wait and see."

"She gonna be good?" Keone replied.

"I hear that she is very good," remarked Ms. Chambers.

On the afternoon of the program, Ms. Chamber announced, "Let's welcome Amanda, the Dancing Storyteller." All the children clapped, except for Keone and his friends.

The Dancing Storyteller stood in front of the 12-year olds, seated on the floor. She was costumed in a sequined leotard and a shimmering cape. Amanda's strong and graceful body, from years of dancing, floated onto the performance platform. Without even speaking, her stature drew attention. She was the vision of "The Little Mermaid" in the story by Hans Christian Andersen.

She began the story slowly. "Far out to Sea, the water is blue as a lovely cornflower." She stretched her arm straight out, looked far off in the distance, and then curled her hands into the shape of a flower. It was similar to Hula in combining song with dance, but this wasn't Hula. The children had never seen a combination of movements like this. They were in awe even though it wasn't hula or hip-hop. Keone and his buddies nudged each other and giggled; they watched to see what she might do next.

Amanda continued telling the story. "And clear as the purest glass," she murmured, as she flexed her palms and spread her arms out in front of her.

"Wow," said Keone. "I'm seeing da glass, just like when surfing da ocean, yeah?

"Ssssh," the girls in the front row said.

Amanda continued, "There grow the most beautiful trees and bushes that sway with the least movement of the water." Gently, she raised her arms overhead and swayed. Except for a few oohs and aahs, the room was silent now; she had captured the interest of all the children, including Keone and the other "tough" boys. They were fascinated. When she portrayed the witch placing an evil spell on the mermaid with a deep curdling laugh, the kids were elated and did the witch laugh with her. Keone did the loudest witch laugh. Everyone was inside the story with her now, concerned for the fate of the Little Mermaid.

At the end of the story, they all clapped. Keone and his pals stomped and did a hip-hop dance for Amanda and the rest of the class to show their appreciation for the storyteller.

Girl in the Hallway

"The soul is healed by being with children."
- Fyodor Dostoyevsky, Russian Novelist and Philosopher

The fourth grade teacher, Ms. Princeton, gave the performer Amanda the high sign to start her "Stories from Africa" program without a hello or even an introduction. In developing these dancing stories, Amanda had taken special training in African Dance. A little appreciation, like a welcome from the teacher, mattered to get a program off to a good start. There was no time to get upset, however; the children in front of her eagerly awaited to see and hear what this barefoot woman, in the bright orange and black get-up with a matching twisted head scarf, had to offer.

Amanda began, "Have you ever pretended to be very, very sad when you weren't even the least bit sad?"

All the children raised their hands in answer to that question, and she called on several that kept their hands up.

"When I don't get what I want, I can really cry. Like this." And when the kid began to cry right on the spot, everybody laughed.

Another pretended to cry like the last kid and said, "I pretend that I am sad when there is a good show on TV and my mom says it's time for bed. Usually, she lets me stay up for the show."

"I know, I know," a tall boy shouted. "I turn down my mouth and squint my eyes and pretend I have a stomach ache when my mother tries to get me to eat broccoli. I hate broccoli."

"Ou,ou, broccoli. Ick!" The other kids understood that one; they stuck out their tongues.

"Oh, you are very good storytellers. So, I guess people believe you then?" remarked Amanda.

"Oh, yeah," the tall boy said. "It works every time."

Everyone laughed and was now in a good mood to hear the folktale, the "Hat Shaking Dance," starring the ill-fated trickster, Anasai the Spider.

Amanda slid into her story, "In this story from Liberia, Africa, Anasai, the spider, goes to his mother-in-law's funeral and carries on so much that people think he is the saddest one there. He even pretends that he is too sad to eat."

"Just like me," said the tall boy.

"Yes, just like you." Again, everyone had a good laugh and pointed a finger at the tall boy.

"The funeral went on for several days with Anasai saying he was so sad that he couldn't eat… but, in truth, he *was* starving. He was about to eat some beans that were cooking over the fire when his friends returned from a hike. To hide the beans he stuck them in his hat. Those beans were burning his scalp. To stand the pain, the only thing he could do was DANCE. Please stand and join me in the Hat Shaking Dance." Amanda started some African drum music and the kids joined her in shaking all over the room and holding their pretend hats of beans on their heads.

It was so much fun for everyone, especially the storyteller who enjoyed dancing with the kids. There were two more stories and then she ended the program. Ms. Princeton called the kids back to their lesson, never looked at or thanked her, or said goodbye as Amanda gathered her stuff. Amanda looked at Ms. Princeton, before she walked out the door; the teacher was busy giving her lesson and never even seemed to notice that the performer was leaving and trying to say "thank you."

In the hallway, Amanda put on her street shoes. *What did I do wrong? I must have offended her in some way. Maybe I wasn't good enough.* She was crushed. She'd put so much effort into the program and the teacher acted like she was a waste of time.

As she was doubting and blaming herself, a girl from the class appeared before her. Like an angel sent from heaven this child with a soft countenance said, "Thank you so much. This was so special for me." The girl placed her hands on her heart and looked into Amanda's eyes with love. Amanda felt she was touching something beyond form, something mystical. What she may have imagined the teacher to be thinking didn't matter at all. Amanda floated out of the building on a cloud.

Hawaiian Girl

"Go confidently in the direction of your dreams.
Live the life you've always imagined."
~ Henry David Thoreau

In the winter of 1972, Catherine James left behind 32 years of chaos, an apartment full of antiques and other valuable items, and bought a ticket to Hawaii. *The weather in San Francisco stinks; it is always foggy and I'm cold. Who needs it? And as for the rest of my life…well, forget that too. It's time to start over again with no attachments to the past.*

Seated on the plane gazing at the expansive Pacific, she visualized palms swaying in the breeze, warm sunshine, gentle waves rolling onto shore, and a life without hassle. She saw herself with a tan, a flower over her ear, wearing a grass skirt. *That is the Me-to-Be.* She had seen the name 'Lei'lani on a post card from Hawaii and liked it. *From now on I am Lei'lani, the Hawaiian Girl.*

Lei'lani didn't have much money to start on a new path; only $40 and it was all in her pocket. *Why worry? I am on my way to Paradise where everything is beautiful, perfect, easy, and blissful.* Lei'lani intended to reach up and out even if it meant going out on a limb; which was perfect, as long as it involved someplace new and exciting. *Onward and outward, I go.*

"Where is the least populated place on the islands?" she asked the stewardess and passengers on the plane, who lived in Hawaii.

They all agreed, "Not a lot of people on Molokai."

"OK, then! That is where I will go."

The locals snickered as Lei'lani laughed joyfully.

"Not much there; you know." The Stewardess whispered and smiled gently at Lei'lani.

"I don't need much; just some peace and quiet." *Here I come, beautiful Molokai, beautiful beaches, beautiful trees, I can feel the sand between my toes; oh, la, la.*

With a portion of her $40, Lei'lani purchased a ticket at the Honolulu airport for a flight on a small commuter flight, directly to Molokai. "Take me to a hotel with grass huts on a beautiful beach," she told the cab driver.

"You got it, Wahine."

"Wahine? That means Hawaiian woman; doesn't it?"

"Yes, now you in Hawaii; you one Hawaiian woman."

"Yes, brother, thank you."

"Mahalo, say Mahalo that mean thank you."

"A big Mahalo to you, brother."

"Bruddah."

"A big Mahalo to you, Bruddah."

"Yep, you one Wahine, now."

When they arrived at the hotel, Lei'lani was humming "The Little Grass Shack" melody and exhilarated. The palm trees seemed to wave to her in the breeze. *Ah, such perfect beauty! Paradise, here I sure am.* She paid the driver and grabbed her backpack.

"Aloha, Wahine."

"Aloha, Bruddah."

After checking into the hotel and putting her suitcase in the grass hut-styled condo, she changed into her bathing suit right away, grabbed a towel, and headed for the serenity of the sand and surf. *Look at that water; feel that sun, ah, so beautiful. I love it.* She flopped down on the towel and felt the warm smooth sand penetrate her skin. She giggled as the ocean lapped at her toes. *Wow! I'm here; this is so right-on.* A big smile spread across her face.

A few minutes later, she heard, "Urrrrrrr….uhhhhhh, bump, screech, bump", a dump truck rumbled up and down the pier offshore. She started up from her towel.

"What? A god damn truck next to this pristine beach?" she shouted. "How could this be? This doesn't fit. What is a dump truck doing in Paradise? I don't need this!" she mumbled. The sunbathers looked up and only laughed as she jumped up, grabbed her towel, and ran towards her hut. In a matter of moments, she had her things and was in a cab back to the airport. She didn't see any office buildings where she might find a typing job, anyway. *Need to manifest, money! I need money and Molokai doesn't look too promising in that respect, either.*

After buying a ticket to Honolulu, she was broke!

Honolulu was a city. She figured she'd find a job there. When she got off the plane in Honolulu, she smelled the sweetness of flowers in the air. "Hey, this is nice. This city is ok."

"Howzit?" A tall, strong, bronze airline porter greeted her, as he unloaded her backpack from the small inter-island plane.

"'Howzit?' What's that you said?

"Means Hi, how's you doing? Howzit, Haole Girl."

"'Haole Girl?' What's that; why do you call me that?"

"Dat means you is one white girl. Ha, Ha."

"Oh, OK. I guess. Hi; I mean howzit? Ha! I wish that I could say I'm OK; but, this Haole Girl is broke and needs to find a job right away."

"Broke! Poor Ting. I going my second job now, delivering pizzas for Chicken Delight. Maybe get you one job there. I'm Jim and you?" he said, extending his hand.

"Lei'lani." She shook his hand.

"So, you make da kind?"

"Da kind what?"

"Pizza!"

"I guess; never did it, but I'll figure it out; I need money."

"No figa; just cook! I take you to town, you meet da boss."

"OK, I guess."

At the restaurant, Lei'lani watched Jim talk with Randy, who looked her up and down and sideways. Loudly, Randy asked, "Is she in trouble?"

Lei'lani shook her head.

"Neh! She clean. She broke, dat's all."

Well, so much for the ceremonies. Soon, Lei'lani was making pizza. A little sloppy at first, but nobody seemed to notice. She figured that she would get the hang of it. *Everything will be OK now; I will be earning money.*

"Where's the bathroom, Randy." Lei'lani asked politely.

"In the back, by the trash." Her boss, Randy, answered harshly, staring at her body.

"By the trash, oh….OK."

Lei'lani pushed open the cruddy door to the can. Three-inch reddish-brown cockroaches ran across and around her feet; they were everywhere, even on the walls. "Yick!" she cried out. "There are a million of them!" She sidestepped to get out of the bathroom and to avoid a glide on one of their backs.

A few of the big brown roaches ran across the pizza prep counter. "Double Yick!"

"Double Yick; what dat, Lei'lani?" Jim asked, returning from a delivery.

"Oh nothing, nothing." Lei'lani reminded herself that she is lucky to have a job.

Lei'lani also took phone orders for pizza. "CA LA Cow what? Could you spell that please? K.A.L.A.K.A.U.A., oh, OK, I got it."

Jim and Randy had a good laugh as she tried to speak and jot down Hawaiian street names. They laughed hysterically as she scrambled the street names and asked for numerous repetitions. She frowned as they hooted 'One Haole Girl'.

"You need a place to stay, Haole Girl? I have one extra room." Randy offered.

"Yeah, I guess."

"It's close to work; you can walk. You don't have car, right?"

"Right on that one."

"Well, then you stay there with me, Haole Girl."

"Well, OK; but, please stop calling me 'Haole Girl'."

"OK; I'll take you home after work."

Ah, money and a room. Cool.

It was a nice enough room; but, soon she would have to sidestep a human cockroach. The second night she was there, she woke up to the handle on her door jiggling. "Who's there?"

"Open the door," Randy slurred.

"Go away; I am sleeping."

The jiggling continued. "Wanna play; have some fun, Haole Girl?

"Gee Whiz! Go away; you can't come in my room in the middle of the night, Cockroach!"

"What you say?"

"Go away, Cockroach. It's late! Go to sleep!"

Finally, the jiggling stopped. *Thank God, he's quit. I'm out of here tomorrow!*

Lei'lani found a room in a house with some other girls. Back at work, she avoided the cockroaches, including the human one. Fortunately there was another manager on duty most of the time, a family man and a Haole Man. He loved to eat the mold off the cheese. *Strange guy, but better than working with Randy.*

Lei'lani improved at taking phone orders. "You live at 453 Ka La Kau A, right; OK!" In the next few months, she focused on learning Hawaiian street names and making pizzas fly. She perfected the Cockroach Two-Step to get out of the bathroom safely and to avoid advances from Randy. She saved money by walking everywhere and savored swimming in the ocean and lying on the beach. She acquired a tan, let her hair grow down to her waist, and wore a flower over her ear. She even used chopsticks better than a fork. Forget the 'Haole Girl'; she was a local girl now. She was groovin' in Hawaii! *Go figa!* She was getting on with her life.

Depth Perception

*"As long as the world is turning and spinning, we're
gonna be dizzy and we're gonna make mistakes."*
~ Mel Brooks

In the middle of the night, Marie Sanders woke up from a nightmare. She'd dreamt that Bob, a guy she knew in Chicago, was stalking up the stairs to her apartment in Hawaii... he was after her. It didn't seem likely that would happen, but she was frightened. It was just a dream; but, it seemed so real. She couldn't keep from asking herself, *Why is he after me? Why would he be here?*

She slid back under the covers and fell asleep again. This time she was in a dentist's chair. As she opened her mouth for the dentist to look at her teeth, she cried out, "Doctor, I've seen too much; don't hurt me."

The Dentist assured her, "It's OK, it's OK. You have depth perception. Use it to see beyond appearances, beyond the pain."

The next morning, she recalled the weird dreams. She was trembling with fear from both of them. Somehow, they seemed related. Her fear turned to anger when she thought about Bob. *I don't need to ever see Bob again, after what he called me in San Francisco. A "ball breaker." The nerve! He had a brain injury and drank screwdrivers for breakfast. The other dream was pretty strange, too. I'd sure like to have depth perception, to see beyond appearances, beyond pain. Wouldn't that be a fine thing?*

Not counting her fitful night, Marie's life seemed to be on the upswing. She had a good waitress job at Penny's Coffee Shop. She could afford the rent of an apartment on the 3rd floor of an art deco building with a view of the Ala Wai Canal. It had a real wood floor and Koa furniture. She loved to dance on the wood floor.

Sipping a cup of hot chocolate, she sat back in a huge rattan chair with Hawaiian print overstuffed cushions. She gazed out her third floor window, mesmerized by the flowing water in the canal. She read for a while and then closed the book to think about what she was doing that day, the first day of a new year. "Happy New Year to me! Here I come, Jimi Hendrix! Life is good." She got up to dress for the Hendrix concert that was going to take place in the Diamond Head Crater. She pulled on a richly patterned burgundy and gold long shirt that she'd made from an East Indian bedspread. *My dancing skirt, yeah.* She drew in and tied the narrow rope in the waistband and threw a loose thin white blouse over her head. Next, she brushed her shiny, long, wavy brown hair, put on beaded gold earrings and a necklace, leather sandals, and dabbed sandalwood oil on her neck, shoulders, and arms. "Ah, lookin' good, Lady," she said aloud to herself in the mirror. She grabbed a beaded embroidered purse and headed out the door for a big day in the Crater. "Here comes the sun". She sang the Beatles song all the way to the bus stop.

In the Diamond Head Crater, Jimi Hendrix's electric guitar and voice blasted out through the sound system.

Marie bobbed her head back and forth and rocked her shoulders, catching the beat as she greeted some people and slipped to the ground to share a joint. She looked around to see what all was happening. She scanned the food and craft booths, and grinned at all the folks having fun at the concert. "This is so cool," she said to the guy next to her.

"Yeah, groovy, man," sang the guy, who handed her a joint that had been circulating. The air got lighter after she took a puff of the weed. She looked at Hendrix, belting out his songs.

Here and there, people were getting up to dance on the grass. Marie rose up and felt herself float and swirl in the breeze. She was ecstatic... high... flying high. A trained dancer, her smooth, skilled movements drew the attention of those around her. Marie loved having an audience. She smiled as she swayed and spun throughout the crowd. Suddenly, she stopped cold. A familiar face in the crowd brought her to a standstill.

It can't be. I must be tripping. She rubbed her eyes and looked again. From several feet away, *he* was smiling at her. "My God, it's Bob from San Francisco." Her words were lost in the noise of the concert. She shivered as their eyes locked. *He is here! I don't want to see him here. But he is here. The dream....*

Cheerfully, Bob got up and teetered towards Marie.

"Hey, Dude, quick, give me a toke," Marie said to a guy sprawled on the ground. She took a long drag, held it, and coughed it out.

"Well, if it isn't Marie!" Bob said with a laugh as he arrived in her face.

Marie's spirits sank in a cloud of apprehension and then she checked herself. *That's foolish. What am I thinking? I am not about fear. After all, it was just a stupid dream. Don't be irrational. He's an old friend. People say all kinds of shit. I must be positive. I will manifest good things. Love, trust, forgive, accept.* A pattern of decorative hearts swirled before her stoned-out eyes.

Between the hearts stood Bob with open arms.

Of course. Love is the answer. "What a surprise!" she said, as she returned the hug.

"The landlady said you'd moved to Hawaii. What a great idea! Thought I'd give it a try."

"Oh yeah, this is the place!"

"Do you live near here?"

"Not real far." With her caution blunted by the weed, Marie wrote her address on a piece of paper and gave it to him. "Come by and 'I'll serve you tea and oranges that come all the way from China'." Marie sang from the Judy Collins' song. After he left, she started shaking. "This is some heavy weed, man," she said to no one in particular.

"Yeah, it's hashish, baby," said the guy sprawled on the ground.

"Hashish?"

"Yeah. It's the buds. It's potent, baby, real potent," the guy said, swiveling his hips.

"Potent? Right," replied Marie, who had landed on a multi-colored planet somewhere out in space.

"Have a seat, Mama, right here by me," the guy said, patting the ground. "You sure can dance, Lady."

"Thanks." Marie stopped listening to him. She stood perfectly still. All she could hear was Jimi Hendrix singing "There must be someway outta here." It was strong message; it was like he was singing to her. Something didn't feel right. She heard the dentist from the dream saying, "You have depth perception. Trust it."

Turning to the guy on the ground, she said, "I'm not feeling good. I have to go."

Marie set out to find the Crater exit. The past seemed to be creeping up on her.

Pretty wasted the next morning, Marie watched the sparkling water in the canal. She had planned to write today. Disturbed by the dreams and a possible connection to reality, she made a concerted effort to pull out the play she had began in Chicago. *It's been a long time since I worked on this.* As she visualized her scenes, she heard a knock at the door. *I don't want to see anybody. I barely have enough energy to write. I don't need anything else to deal with.* She opened the door, and there was Bob in wrinkled clothing.

His timing is terrible and he looks awful. Guess I'll have to let him in. "Oh, Bob. Hi. Oh, umm, come in. I'll… I'll put some water on to boil for tea. Have a seat. Umm . . . would you like some oranges? Ha, ha, ha. I was just working on my play. You know, the one that I started in Chicago." *I'll serve him some tea and then get rid of him.*

"Sure. You're a writer. I-I-I remember," Bob stuttered.

Drinking tea and looking the place over, Bob mumbled, "You've got a nice—a nice place here." Staring squarely at her with dull eyes, he stated, "It's good—good to see you again."

Marie ignored Bob's demeanor and stuttering, and answered, "Yeah, I really like being on the Ala Wai. And it's close to my job. Nice to see you, too, here in Hawaii. Wow!"

With eyes downcast, he asked, "Oh, you—you are working. Where?"

"I'm a waitress at Penney's...It's...umm... in the shopping center." It took her a while to get it out. She thought right away, *I shouldn't have told him that...*

There was a long pause in the conversation. Bob was fidgeting; his face contorted. He was obviously perplexed. Marie began to tremble. She recalled... *it's the accident, his screwed thinking.* His knotted brow and wrenched expression were quite familiar to her now. Marie was tired, but not stoned—reality was setting in.

"What's going on?" Marie questioned apprehensively. She realized now that she should never have invited him to come here.

Bob dropped his head to his chest and whined, "I'm so l-l-lonely."

Worse, you are pathetic! "Oh, umm... ahhuh... I . . . I'm sorry to hear that." *I wish he'd leave.*

"We could live together."

"What! Oh... No... no... no... that would never work. You can't crash here."

"But, I'm lonely," he complained. "I can't be alone anymore."

"NO! I'm sorry! I'm not sharing my place with anyone. I need my own space!"

Bob arose slowly and slumped as he walked out the door, leaving it ajar. Marie jumped up, closed it, and secured the latch. *At least he is going down the stairs and away, instead of up the stairs, as I'd dreamt.*

Sapped, Marie remembered something else Bob had said to her, back in Chicago, "You're too independent. You are a threat to men," he'd complained. *Why, oh why did I give him my address? I am glad I said NO. That is that... I am rid of him.*

Marie took a couple of deep breaths and turned her attention back to her play. In the last scene of the first act, there was a rape. She saw Bob's knotted face as it had been earlier that day. He **was** coming up the stairs, in anger, coming after her.

Her reverie was interrupted by a pounding on the door. He was back. Leaving the latch in place, she opened the door only slightly. She gasped. There was Bob, scowling. It wasn't a dream. Panicked, she cried out, "I'm busy now, Bob! You can't come in!" When Marie tried to push the door shut, he used his weight to shove it open. The latch snapped.

He stalked into the room and pushed her back. He ripped off one side of her blouse, from the shoulder down to her waist. Startled, she ran out the door. He grabbed her and held onto her. She pulled away. She was hanging over the railing. She looked down. It was a long way to the ground, 3 stories, *My God!* She ducked, ran, and banged on her neighbor's door.

Bob was on her heels, grabbing her arm again. Inside the neighbor's apartment, she straightened her arm, putting him at a distance. She heard the dentist again from her dream telling her, *'It's OK; it's OK; you have depth perception; use it to see beyond appearances, beyond the pain.'* *He is a frightened lonely little boy; not a threat.* Miraculously, she heard herself sweetly say, "Bob, we have been friends for a long time; this will ruin our friendship." It worked; Bob's passion dissipated. He let go and walked out the door.

Quickly, Marie ran to the phone to call the police and blurted into the receiver, "A man just tried to rape me. He is wearing jeans and a plaid shirt. He teeters when he walks. He has brain damage and is an alcoholic. He is walking down the Ala Wai towards the bridge. His name is Bob."

"They are going to pick him up, Sally." Marie told her neighbor, a middle-aged woman, who had been frozen in one spot since the incident started.

Sally suddenly came back to life. "Where did you meet that nut case? Marie, he could have killed both of us."

"Everything will be OK now; don't be scared. I'm sorry I had to burst in here like that. We are safe now. They will surely put him away for good when they see how disturbed he is."

"But, where did you get hooked up with him?"

"In Chicago; he lived upstairs in my apartment building. I thought he was cute at first, but later found out that he had brain damage. He was a physicist before he took LSD and got in a car accident."

"That's a pity."

"Yeah, I used to feel sorry for him; but, not anymore."

"No way, Marie; a woman needs to take care of herself. Watch who you get involved with, Marie; be more careful."

"You're right Sally; that's what I need to do, for sure."

Sally opened the door for Marie to leave.

"Thank you, Sally," Marie said giving her neighbor a hug. "We're safe now."

A few days later, back at work at Penney's restaurant, Marie placed some pancakes before a customer at the counter. Out of the corner of her eye, she saw Bob. *No, it can't be; he's in jail.*

"Good morning, Marie." Bob said.

Marie's mind raced, *He's been released from jail!* "Bob!"

He glared at her. *Of course, he knows I had him arrested.*

Marie released the cup of coffee for the customer onto the counter. It spilled, but she didn't stop to clean it up. She darted to the kitchen.

"What happened? You're white as a ghost," one of the waitresses remarked as Marie grabbed her purse and started to run off.

"I've got to go. Tell the Supervisor that I had to leave; someone is after me," Marie muttered and escaped through the kitchen door.

Marie returned to her apartment briefly to fill her backpack and book a plane back to Chicago.

She knocked on Sally's door before leaving. "I'm taking off, Sally. Bob is out of jail."

"Oh, no. "I'm sorry to see you go, Marie. What a shame all of this happened," Sally said.

"It's awful! I'm sorry that you got involved in it. Do you need some stuff? I can't take everything with me."

"Sure. What do you have?"

"Look around and take what you want, Sally. The landlady can have the rest. I left her a note. Would you please give her the key?"

"Sure. Where will you go?"

"Back to the Mainland for awhile. I need to get my bearings."

"Are you coming back to Hawaii?" Sally asked.

"Hopefully; time will tell. I need to chill out for a while. Gotta go now, Sally. I don't want to be late for my plane."

"Keep in touch. You know where I live."

"I will, Sally and thanks for being there for me."

The High Road

"All good things are wild and free."
~ Henry David Thoreau

One day on the bus, a thin guy with a crop of black curls, fine features, and a dark sexy mole on his left cheek, winked at Jane Saunders. He spotted her when he first got on and made a point of sitting next to her, like she was his long lost friend. "Good day, lovely lady." It was nice to have someone smile at her after all she'd been through. She had fled from Los Angeles to Honolulu to get away from her dysfunctional family and an oppressive marriage, only to return to L.A., after someone tried to rape her. When she sought solace from her mother, her mother gave her money to stay in a motel. She was waitressing to earn enough to return to Hawaii. She hated living on the Mainland; she missed the warm beautiful beaches and waving palm trees on the islands. She would go to Maui this time. She had had enough of cities.

She smiled and then looked out the window; but, she thought *he is kind of cute.* She couldn't help smiling. Well, she could have and maybe should have, but she didn't. And then, as the bus bounced along, and veered to the next stop, he peered around her shoulder into her face.

"Are you an artist?" he asked, matching her grin.

She couldn't help having another look at him, and he was, after all, calling for her attention. "You mean artist as in painter?"

"No, not necessarily." He looked her up and down and then gazed deeply into her eyes. "You look like a creative type."

Flattered, Jane brushed back her long, flowing hair and smiled right at him. "Well… I do write and dance."

"I knew it. What do you write, lady?"

"Plays." Jane looked at him and he was winking again and nodding his head. *He seems very interested in me and what I am about.*

"Ah ha! So do I."

"You're kidding!" Jane exclaimed.

"No lie. I write for a bunch of actors, and I am an actor too."

"Really? You've had your stuff produced?"

"Yes, several of them. I can introduce you around. We always need fresh material."

"Oh! Really, that's far out, brother."

"Where do you live? I'll stop by sometime and give you some feedback on your writing."

Jane looked down and frowned. "In a crummy motel."

"A crummy motel? Why?"

"About all I can afford right now."

"Hm… if you're interested, there's a room for rent where I live in West Hollywood. The house is full of artistic types. You'd like it there. Cheap, too."

"Really? Great!" Things seemed to be looking up for Jane.

"I try my best to fill a need, when I see one. What did you say your name was?"

"I didn't. It's Jane. And yours?"

"You can call me Lover Boy."

Jane moved into the West Hollywood rooming house and jumped into bed with Lover Boy. He bit instead of kissed. She quickly had enough of the carnivorous Romeo, and he also had a jealous girlfriend with a sting. "Stay away from my man or I'll kill you," the girlfriend warned.

"No problem, lady." The girlfriend had nothing to worry about as far as Jane was concerned.

In another room in the house lived Sandy, quite a friendly guy or gal; the time of day or mood induced the change in persona. He was only a guy part of the time; at night, he let his hair down. One evening, he invited Jane to his room. After they smoked a joint, he excused himself. As he exited, he set the stage for his return by switching on a black light to facilitate his transformation into the female gender. It was a new experience for Jane; she was amused.

If ever a human could fly, it was this guy. When he returned, under the cast of the black light, Sandy fluttered towards her in a floral mini dress, all 6 feet of him. In the black light, the flowers on his dress glowed bright chartreuse and violet. Through the slit in the neckline his hairy chest protruded and blended with the hair on his head that now draped gracefully over his shoulders. Jane was pleasantly high and ready to be entertained. Ah, the power of forgetfulness as only Pot can perpetrate!

He swished his long hair to the other side and tucked the skirt of his mini dress under his hairy thighs as he sat down next to Jane. He smiled sweetly and wrapped a comforting arm around her like a big mother bird. Not really a substitute for a real mother's arm; Jane took shelter and solace in his protective embrace like the little lost bird that she was.

Another transvestite lived there; he was known as "The Queen." The Queen was a bitch, swaying his hips in his long silky gown and slinky fur wrap. She steered clear of that one. She didn't want to trip on his train or be slashed by his cape.

The Hollywood House was one bizarre trip after another; and not just for Jane. In the middle of the night, Jane awoke to a loud siren in the driveway. Sadly, the one straight guy in the house besides Lover Boy, in which weirdoes ruled, had met his end. *I guess he just didn't fit in, didn't belong here in the first place, which could have been a blessing if he hadn't taken it out on himself.* The ambulance came to take him away after he ingested a whole bottle of Tylenol.

The suicide was a wakeup call for Jane, however. She had to ask herself, *What in the world am I doing here? I need to get out of this Web of Weirdoes. I don't belong here. I need to find another place to live. I need to get back to Hawaii! Soon, I will have the money to do it!*

At the fancy fish house on Restaurant Row, she worked alongside a wiry bleached blond gal named Patricia, Pat for short. Pat was a chain smoker and had a sexy son, also named Pat. Jane left the bizarre rooming house and moved in with the Pat Group.

Unfortunately, she had traded one bizarre situation for another. Pat, the sexy son, looked like a normal everyday guy in the daytime, but, at night… he was a crook. He was a member of a gang that raided the meat section of markets, while high on LSD. The gang members weren't poor or starving; they scored steaks for kicks.

One night, when Pat was exceptionally appealing, he looked at her lovingly and said, "Let's go trippin' baby. Have some Acid." He held up a vial of cloudy water.

"Acid? What's that?"

"It's a good time, a new universe, colors, music. It's exciting… a trip to the stars."

"Wow. Let's go." Anything was better than her current reality of busting her butt at the fish house and living in smoggy L.A.

Well, LSD, now that was something new and different to Jane and a lot more potent than marijuana. It helped her forget painful thoughts of her family and oppressive ex-husband; but, it brought new problems. She indulged because she was curious to see what it felt like; or, more aptly what it didn't feel like, since it obliterated her feelings.

Jane was totally unprepared for what was about to hit her. Strung out on Pat's bed, bright colors and patterns rearranged themselves non-stop like a giant kaleidoscope on the screen in her brain. When she got up, her head was spinning and she lost her balance completely. She had to hold onto the walls to make it to the bathroom. *I am wiped out… barely alive. I want to sleep and wake up in reality—wherever that is. I have to get away from this scene. I need stability. Oh, Hawaii, if I were only there now.*

In a few days, Jane announced her exit plan, including Pat, the son. She was ready for the actual trip. "Pat, do you want to go to Hawaii?"

"I've never been there."

"It is beautiful. Better than an Acid Trip."

"Better than an Acid Trip? Really?"

"Yeah, a major improvement."

"I'm sorry you had a bad trip, Baby. Let's go to Hawaii. I hear they have great buds there."

"I want to go to Maui. Better than Honolulu, and I hear that you can sleep on the beach free."

"Really, for free?"

"Yeah, for free."

"I'm in, Baby."

So, they made reservations to go to Maui and filled their backpacks with summer duds. On the plane, they befriended Jerry, a guy with a beard and long hair. They knew he was a hippie, like them.

"Do you know where we can sleep on the beach on Maui?" Pat asked.

"Sure, man. Take your bodies to McKenna Beach. There are a lot of cool people hanging there."

"Right on! Where is it?"

"On the south side of the island, past the town of Kihei."

"How do you get there?"

"You can hitch a ride there. Everyone hitches on Maui."

"Are you headed there?"

"No, I'm homesteading out in Paia with my old lady."

"What about the buds, dude? They have good buds on Maui?"

"Yeah, real good... hashish."

"What is hashish?" Pat asked, too loudly.

"Shush! There might be fuzz on the plane. It's the best buds, man. You'll know it when you smoke it. It goes in a pipe," he whispered.

"Super fine, man. Thanks for the info." They touched hands in the Hi sign.

Jane and Pat settled back into their seats with visions of sun-splashed beaches, turquoise waters, and the greater imminent world of island hashish.

When they arrived on Maui, they caught a ride to McKenna Beach from Hansen Road near the airport.

"Wow, man, this is cool!" said Pat, as his eyes followed the beach line from the car.

"I told you," replied Jane, gaping at Maui's beauty.

"Maui's da kine," the driver said, offering them a toke of Pot.

"Thanks, man. This is my kind of place," Pat said to the driver.

At dusk, the bonfires were lit when Pat and Jane arrived at the clothes-optional McKenna Beach. A couple of freshly rolled thick joints were being passed around a circle of the partially-clad beach squatters. The sweet smell of marijuana blended with the pungent mesquite burning in the bonfire. The sound of waves rolling onto the shore provided background music to the cozy setting. Smiles were exchanged around the circle to greet the newcomers, but everyone was too high and laid back to carry on a conversation. A friendly, bare-chested, buxom young woman arose and came over to them. She motioned for them to get up and then pointed to a spot where they could spread out their sleeping bags.

"Whoa!" exclaimed Pat, fixated on the woman's ample breasts.

"Must be the good stuff! I'm ridin' HIGH!" he said, tickling Jane and patting her butt.

"I gather you like Maui," she responded, bumping up against him.

"It's the finest, Baby. Let's cuddle up."

"There are sure a lot of people around here. Not too private."

"What are a couple hundred hippies, when you're one of them? Everybody must do it out in the open." Pat whispered.

"Yes, sure. But I feel a little strange about it."

"We can zip our sleeping bags together and get it on inside."

"Well, OK. Sounds like it would work."

"Ready?"

"Yeah, but I'd like to shower first," stated Jane.

"I don't think that is an option."

"You can't bathe here?"

"Well, there is probably a cold beach shower somewhere. Why don't you wait until the morning when you can spot where it is?"

"Cold shower?"

"Come on, baby. Let's do it," Pat said, impatiently.

"OK, OK."

In no time, they unfolded and zipped together their sleeping bags and crawled inside.

"I need to pee. Where do I pee?" asked Jane.

"There is probably a beach bathroom somewhere."

"Where?"

"How do I know? It's too dark to see. Go anywhere. Go find a place and hurry back. I've got something waiting just for you."

"Hold onto that. I'll be right back," Jane said laughing. She darted off into the bushes.

Jane wasn't sure where to go, so she just picked a spot in the brush where no one could see her. Her nose told her that she wasn't the first one to use the area. *Gross!*

The next morning, they awoke to an angry-eyed stoned guy with scabs standing above them, cursing. "OK, Dude, give me back my bread."

"What, bread?" questioned Pat, rubbing his eyes.

Another guy, equally stoned, with scabs all over his arms joined the first one. "You heard him, Creepo! Give him back the money you stole from him."

Jane awoke, startled. "What's going on?"

"I saw you go into the bushes, lady, where I hid my money. It's gone this morning. You gave it to your man!"

"No, no, I didn't. I just peed in the bushes. I didn't see any money. What are those scabs from on your bodies?"

"Staph."

"What's it from? How did you get it?"

"Goes with the territory. Come on, tell your man to give us the money you found."

"She didn't give me anything. She just went to the bathroom."

"Cough it up, bud."

When the scabbed guys turned to go get some more guys, Pat whispered to Jane, "We're outta here." They quickly slid into their jeans, stood up, grabbed their backpacks and ran for it.

When they reached the highway, they stuck out their thumbs. "That was a close call," Jane said.

"Too close for me. Those guys could have leveled me and taken all my money. Let's go back to L.A."

"What? We just got here! I have been scared away before. I am not leaving again. The Mainland is not for me."

"I've seen enough, thanks. You don't know what will happen in a foreign place like this."

"Foreign place? This is Hawaii! It's part of the United States. Don't freak on me."

"There is a whole ocean between here and where I feel safe. I am going home while I still have enough money to do it!"

"I'm staying here where it is warm and beautiful."

Pat was flabbergasted. "Huh? Well, good luck to you, chick. Nice knowing you. I see someone slowing down to give us a ride. You coming?"

"No."

"No? Really?"

Jane nodded.

"OK. Goodbye, Jane. Beware of goons with scabs."

"Yeah. OK. I will," Jane said, waving goodbye to Pat. "Goodbye, Mama's Boy."

Alone on the highway, she prayed for safety and gathered her courage. *Dear God, I know that you are here, guiding me. It will work out. I know it will. It has to. I am happy again. I am in Hawaii, where I want to be. How could I not be happy in Hawaii? Amen and Hallelujah.*

The Free Spirit

"I am homesick for a place where silence is the only language, love is the only religion, and freedom is not something to be fought for..."
~ Samiha Totanji, Author

"You may not always end up where you thought you were going, but you will always end up where you were meant to be."
~ *Jessica Taylor*

It was Maui 1973: Hippies' Paradise! "Turn on, Tune in, and Drop out." Maui the New Frontier! Jolene Andrews renamed herself Maya, after the spinning Hindu goddess of change. After a dead-end relationship and the loss of her 9-5 boring job, she was a liberated lady, ready for transformation. She figured she might be entitled to some unemployment money to give her time to figure out the rest of her life and have unlimited fun while doing it.

Wailuku was the center of business on Maui and the location of the State Unemployment Office. She stood in a long line for her turn to make her application.

"I'd like to apply for unemployment," Maya told the receptionist.

"Do you live on Maui?"

"I just got here yesterday."

"Do you have an address?"

"Not yet."

"You will need to get an address first."

"Do you know where I can rent a room?"

"There is a bulletin board at the health foods store on Vineyard Avenue. You might find something there."

"Where is Vineyard Avenue? Far from here?"

"No, just two blocks that way and then go to the bottom of the hill."

"Ok, thanks, I'll be back in a few days."

* * *

"Frankie Jones's Crash Pad, sliding scale, nightly," stated the notice on the bulletin board in the health foods store. *Maybe I can stay there a few nights, while I look for a permanent place.* She chomped on a granola bar as she jotted down the address.

"Where can I find this place?" she asked the cashier at the Heart and Earth Store.

"Oh, it's just a few blocks over that way, sister. It's a little white house between two office buildings."

"Thanks, sister." Maya bought some juice and headed over.

A clean-shaven straight-looking guy with short hair answered the door.

"Is Frankie around?" asked Maya.

"C'est moi."

"Are you French? I speak French."

"No, it's just my shtick. I'm from New York."

"Oh, really? I'm from L.A. We have shtick there, too. Hollywood, you know. So, are *you* really Frankie, the guy who runs this place?"

"In the flesh."

"I thought you'd be a hippie."

"I am probably in that category."

"But you don't look like a hippie…. I mean you don't have a beard or long hair and your clothes are ironed."

"Looks are deceiving."

"So it seems."

"What can I do for you, sweetheart?"

"I'd like a place to take off and set down this heavy backpack, and I do need a place to sleep for a couple of nights."

"Come on in. I've always got a place for a lovely lady like you. Here, let me help you take that thing off."

"Thanks, Frankie. Could I bother you for a glass of water?" Without hesitation, Frankie fetched her a glass of water.

"Sure, here you go," he said, handing her the filled glass.

"Whew, it's really hot out there."

"It's *cool* in here, baby… if you know what I mean. Have a look around. Ah… what did you say your name was?"

"I didn't. I am Maya, the Goddess."

"Ah, a goddess. I am entranced. Maya, will you join me in smoking a joint?" he asked, lighting up.

"Hey, yeah, this is where my party begins. I'm free, free, free on beautiful Maui." She took a few long, deep inhales of the weed, and soon found it easy to let her cares tumble away.

"Let me show you around, Maya. I think you'll like the place."

Maya floated in his shadow as he took her around his house from the old plantation days. He had converted the living room into a Head Shop. On sale were commissioned art objects along with hashish pipes, rolling papers, rock concert posters, and the like. Frankie had a lot of irons in the fire… not all of them were legal.

"This is *very cool*. How much do you charge?"

"It's negotiable."

"I don't have a lot of money."

"Don't worry about it," he said as he opened the back door and pointed at the outdoor showers. "Added some extras."

Some other crashers wandered in, starting a non-stop circulation of marijuana joints.

* * *

In the next few months of collecting unemployment, Maya was stoned most of her waking hours. She clicked with Frankie, and when he was entertaining other ladies, she threw her sleeping bag in whatever spot was empty. She wasn't attached to him or any guy or anything.

Drugs of all sorts were plentiful in this house and beyond, even out where the cows grazed. Maya had never seen Hana, the land of cows, on the East side of Maui. One day, she joined a group of crashers headed for the pastureland under a giant cross in Hana. Psychedelic caps bloomed out of the bovine pies there. It was Magic 'Shroom (Mushroom) Time!

The narrow two, sometimes one, lane, 50-mile highway to Hana meandered back and forth for miles. Lush ferns, bamboo, and other tropical plants hugged the landscape, and waterfalls poured from every crevice along the way.

"Exquisite. Far out, man," declared Maya.

"Outrageous," someone else said. "What a trip, man."

"I am staying in this place forever. This is Paradise," said the driver.

There was no need to hurry along this road. They stopped frequently to let cars coming from the other direction go by. It was an opportunity to get out and soak in the ponds and splash in the waterfalls, as they explored the flora and fauna in paradise.

Before reaching Hana, they stopped at Wainapanapa Bay. "This is so far out!" Maya shouted, flying out of the car to see the beach. She stumbled down to and along the rocky black sand beach and up the black lava cliffs. She was dazzled by the glistening sea and the contrast of white leaves on the path against the black rock. There were seabirds everywhere on the narrow trail padded with the smooth long white leaves from the pandanus trees. *This is surely heaven.* On the other side of the bay, she could see waves crashing and shooting up out of blow holes. "Magnificent!" was all she could say. The water was too rough to swim and one of the guys suggested, "Let's investigate those caves."

"Caves? Where?" Maya questioned.

"Right behind us."

"Wow, under those bushes?"

"Yeah, baby. Let's go."

The group, including Maya, tramped through the caves that were big enough to live in, and hippies did that, of course, nature children that they were.

"Looks like this one is taken," said one of the women. "The shelves are packed with household stuff." The cave structure felt private and enveloped them with a sense of comfort. It was quiet and peaceful in there; only the sound of the waves crashing was audible.

"Beats Frankie's Crash Pad or sleeping on the street," said one the guys. They are living naturally, like native Hawaiians." It all looked perfectly acceptable to them. "Wow, far out man," sighed Maya. "Way to go."

A splendid morning it was. After a few tokes on a fresh joint, they were "reloaded" for their afternoon journey to the land of cow pies.

They passed through the quiet verdant town of Hana. Maya could feel the heat and humidity of Eastern Maui flare out of the larger-than-life profuse foliage when the driver made a sharp right turn and rambled up a dirt incline to the big cross. The hunt was on. Not much of a hunt; the mushrooms were everywhere, just waiting to be gathered and consumed.

Each mushroom had a unique design on its cap. Maya ran her finger along the smooth surface of one with a spiral motif. *Ah, a spiral for my spiritual evolution!* Like Alice in Wonderland, she thought she heard the mushroom say "Eat Me." So, she did, without hesitation. *Will I expand and fill the sky now?*

She took a few bites. It tasted like a regular mushroom, but of course, once ingested the results were dramatically different. Her everyday thoughts, already well on their way out, evaporated in the breeze as she lay back on the lush grass and gazed at the drifting cumulus clouds overhead. *Yes, I do feel 10-feet tall and am filling the hillside with my joy.*

That night marked the Annual Aloha Festival on Hana Beach. The residents of Hana looked forward to it and planned it a year in advance. There was a traditional parade, artist booths, and a huge barbeque. The locals looked with scorn at the hippies attending their event, but Maya and the rest of the group didn't notice that they were not particularly welcome. Maya was, in fact, totally absorbed in watching a hippie guy gesticulating towards the clouds in the sky. She wondered what he was seeing in them. Several locals passed him and shook their heads. He seemed to be having as much fun as she had earlier in the day when she gazed at the clouds.

"Who is that? What is he doing?" she asked Tony, one of the guys on the trip.

"He's called Jack 'Fingers.' He communicates with the cosmos through his hands."

"You know him? The cosmos? Wow. I know just where he's coming from. I've got to talk to him. What he's doing is beautiful, so rhythmic."

"Hi there, Jack. I'm Maya."

He looked toward her for a moment. His eyes were ethereal, pale, and blank. "Maya, huh? Glad to meet you. Do you hear it?"

"Hear it?"

"Yes, the music in the spheres."

"Yes, brother, I dig."

Maya stood back to watch and "hear" the sounds of the spheres through his lyrical interchange with the universe. She was enjoying watching Jack 'Fingers' do his thing, when a police officer, accompanied by some irritated Hana residents, started berating him.

"Come on, bud, you can't do that around here." A gigantic local guy started to muscle him.

Maya grabbed Tony and some of the other guys to help. "The police are trying to bust Jack 'Fingers.' The locals are going to beat him up."

When they got close, they heard the cop say, "I said stop that funny stuff with your hands."

Oblivious, Jack kept waving his hands to the cosmos as if he didn't hear the cop or see the annoyed people around him.

"I said stop that! Hana is a small town. Behave yourself, nutcase."

"Please, Officer. Don't arrest him. He's not causing any harm," Tony said.

"He's just having fun!" Maya chimed in.

"Yeah? Fun, huh! Why don't you doped up dirty hippies go home?"

"We are home," they responded, in unison. "We live on Maui."

"Go back to your real home, the Mainland! And take a bath while you're there."

"We'll watch him, Officer. Please don't lock him up."

"OK. But I'm warning you, I want you hippies out of Hana tomorrow. This is a peaceful town. You're crashing our event." The cop directed the onlookers in another direction.

"Yes, peace. Peace, brother. We all want peace."

They wanted to make the peace sign, but they knew he wasn't too fond of hand gestures.

"I'm not your brother," the cop called over his shoulder. "No way am I related to any grimy hippie."

"We'll be gone tomorrow. We promise."

"If you aren't, I'll lock you up in da kine."

Of course, they knew he meant jail. *Imagine that. We weren't breaking any laws or anything,* Maya observed.

The band of hippies took Jack to a less conspicuous place, pointing out to him that he could see the clouds better over on the cliff. And there they partied and matted down in the tall grass, without worrying about the fuzz.

Maya was fascinated by Jack. 'I love the clouds, too, Jack." She told him.

"Far out, lady! Come and visit me in Kanaio sometime. Wait 'till to you see the clouds up there!"

"Are the clouds up there different?"

"Oh, yeah! It's very windy. They continually change shape as they dance in the wind."

"Groovy! I've got to see that. I am a dancer. I'd love to dance in the wind."

"Ah! Then you must come and visit me. I fixed up an old church there. You can see it from the road. I live in a small house next to the church."

"In a church, far out! I will visit you as soon as I get settled." *Settled?* Maya wondered when that would be.

Maya returned to Frankie's Crash pad in Wailuku exhausted from the trip. *Why do drugs always wipe you out?* There was a knock at the door. *I really don't want to see anyone. I'm drained.* Maya dragged herself to the door.

"Is this Frankie's Crash Pad?"

"Yeah."

A burly red-haired woman pushed her way past Maya into the house. "I'm Calamity. I'll be here for a few days."

"There are no spots right now."

"Are you the owner of this place? I thought it was a guy."

"No. I'm not. But I'm staying here, and I know that the bedrooms are full."

"That's OK. I don't need a bedroom. I'll sleep in the living room."

"But..."

The brash red-head was no longer listening. Bang! Bang! Calamity, so aptly named, was slamming every cabinet in the house looking for who knows what. Catastrophe was in the air.

"Where's the food? Isn't there any food in this house?"

"Most of us eat out. Pick up a bite here and there."

"Hm! Where's the coffee? I'd settle for a cup of java."

"None, right now. Sorry."

She glared at Maya, who backed off towards her bedroom which was across from the kitchen. *I'm so tired. I don't need this.*

The next morning when Maya woke up, her head was itching like crazy. She began scratching her scalp. "Eh! There are god-dam bugs in my hair! Who slept in my bag while I was gone?" she asked loudly. A couple of other crashers in the room groaned and turned over. It was too early for them to wake up.

Maya continued scratching. *I've got to go to the drug store and get something! Shit! I must have lice!*

Calamity was flat out in the living room/store area. Frankie was gone for a few days and no one was going to rat on that lady.

I have been here too long. I need to get out of this place soon. It's nuts!

After a few treatments with some salve, her scalp stopped itching. She had to dump her old sleeping bag and buy a new one. And she didn't want to put it down on the floor of the crash pad, that was for sure. So she bundled it up and set it on a shelf.

Maya began to doubt that she was in paradise with everything that was happening. She wished she could find some peace somewhere. *I anticipated that my life would be easy on Maui. But it seems every day is filled with unwelcome challenges and disappointments. I can afford to rent a room, but rentals are scarce. Living out of my backpack or in a crash pad isn't for me. It's too restrictive. I need space.*

While she was having tea in the kitchen of the crash pad, pondering her unsettled life, a local guy came in and sat down at the table.

"Howzit, lady?" he asked with a flirtatious smile.

"Could be better. Who are you? What are you doing here? Are you crashing here?"

Speaking in Pidgin English, he said, "No, I come get one packet da kine from Frankie."

"Oh. I think he's still in Honolulu. Where do you live?"

"Oh, me? Live Kaupo side."

"Kaupo? Isn't that the gap of Haleakala Crater? Do people live on the gap?" Maya asked.

"Yeah! It's one ranch."

"Are you a cowboy?"

"Me, paniolo? No."

"What's that, paniolo?"

"Paniolo, cowboy, same ting."

"What's it like in Kaupo? What does it look like?"

"Nice, Kaupo... up country, you know. Wide open spaces. Have one house there. To-tal-ly quiet, no lights, no traffic. My house ... gap beautiful. See ocean. You come, yah? Got one extra room."

"You're kidding! Really?"

"No kid you. Room for you." He smiled broadly and laughed.

"I came to Hawaii to find peace, beauty, and quiet. And this crash pad isn't it! I need to be free."

Smiling and winking, he continued, " Kaupo, to-tal-ly quiet ... crater ... ocean ... beautiful ... ocean. No noise...."

This was what Maya had been seeking since she left L.A.

"Wow man, sounds perfect! Far out! Yeah, sure, I'll come. I love nature. What's your name?"

"Crazy Guy."

Maya burst out laughing, "Crazy Guy?"

"I like have fun. Dat's why day call me dat."

"Nothing wrong with having fun. No matta now. Crazy is cool."

"Very cool, dat's me." Crazy Guy stood up, turned around, and posed. "What you call you self?"

"Maya."

"Maya. What kind name is dat? Some kind of bird, or someting?"

"A Hindu goddess who dances out new forms of life."

"Ha, Ha, whew! Heavy, lady."

Maya kept thinking, *He is really cute.*

In a short while, Frankie returned from Honolulu with a new stash of weed. He stood in the doorway, in the same spot for fifteen minutes.

"Hey, Frankie," Maya called out.

He grinned into space and remained silent, occasionally swaying back and forth.

Is this an act? Maya wondered. *He told me that he had been on Broadway as a singer, dancer, and actor. He must be acting now. Great show, he looks frozen in place.*

"Hey, Frankie. What's up? It's me, Maya. Earth to Frankie."

No answer.

He must have had training as a mime. He doesn't budge. He doesn't even appear to be breathing. He's either really a good mime or something. Maya stared at him, waiting for him to take a step. *I'm beginning to see that it is more like "something."*

Frankie's real money came from drugs, everything from grass to the hard stuff. He looked like a normal everyday guy. But he a bad habit; he shot heroin. He appeared to be sailing out on some wave, somewhere.

At long last, he finally raised a hand, smiled broadly, and uttered a melodic and drawn out, "Hiiiiiiii." Slowly, he panned the room.

"Welcome back, Frankie." Maya laughed with Crazy Guy, Calamity, and the other awakened crashers who were sitting around watching "Frankie in La La Land."

When Frankie came down from his high on heroin, Maya informed him she was leaving.

"What? Where are you going?"

"Out to Kaupo with Crazy Guy."

"Oh, I see."

"No, no, it's not like that. I just need quiet, some space. I love the country."

"Yeah? It can get pretty noisy here. Well, don't forget me, OK? I am here if you want me. You are special to me. I would take care of you, be good to you. Never throw you out."

What he said made her wonder about the next step that she was taking. But she had had enough of the crash scene, along with the lice. *Too much already.*

Crazy Guy waited in the car while she stuffed her things in her backpack. He didn't help her, just opened the trunk for her to throw it in with his fishing gear and other junk. She was out of the loud crash pad and traveling with Crazy Guy to his "to-tal-ly quiet … crater … ocean … beautiful … ocean. No noise … pad on the gap." It may have been all those things, but that wasn't saying it was a safe place to be or that Crazy Guy wasn't the perfect name for him.

Kaupo was a remote, beautiful Hawaiian settlement on the gap of Haleakala Crater. Maya, a haole, would be a novelty there. On her first day, without delay, some of the rough and ready paniolos came to visit Crazy Guy to assess the haole girl. Friendly, strong, and handsome dudes they were, and the kind who don't take "no" for an answer. One German/Hawaiian paniolo in particular stared at Maya a lot, like he was shopping for something on a store shelf. She was relieved when they left. She didn't like being gawked at like that. She decided to steer clear of them and just enjoy herself in nature.

Every day, Maya took long walks on the dirt country road in front of the house. It was the best part of her day. The town of Kaupo was formed from an ancient lava flow that poured out of the mountain into the sea. Every winter, when it rained hard, the road washed out, so it remained rugged. On one side of Haleakala Crater was lush Hana and on the other side was desert. Maya watched the downpour of rain at sunset that swept across the gap from the tropical rain forests of Hana to the desert. *There it is. I am beholding perfect beauty.* She watched as the falling sheet of water dissipated and created a magnificent double rainbow. The multi-colored arc filled the sky from the tip of Haleakala Crater, 10,000 feet up, all the way down to the ocean, below the Kaupo cliffs. *This is the best. How lucky I am to be here. Free at last.* She meandered beneath the bands of color, looking into the faces of black and white sleek cows grazing in the rolling pastures next to the narrow bumpy road. The wind lifted the bottom of her long skirt as she stood on the crest of a hill, looking down at the ocean below the lava outcroppings. She was in heaven; happy and peaceful at last in the splendor of Kaupo. She felt the joy reserved for a goddess. The house was always dark when she returned. She felt around for the matches, struck one, and lit a kerosene lamp, just like they did in the old days. *I feel like a pioneer woman. It is a simple and beautiful life.* She was comforted as she read by the mellow golden light of the lamp that didn't create a glare like electric light did. It was so quiet. *The last two weeks have been perfect.*

Had she found it? Would this peace and freedom at last? Maya assumed so; but, she should have paid better attention to the facts. NO, it couldn't and didn't last, of course, given the proximity of the paniolos and their unsettling visit. One night when she returned from one her sunset walks, she lit the lamp and jumped back. *Something is crawling up my arm. It's coming towards my face.* With her hand, she whisked off an 8-inch creeping centipede and flung it across the room. "There!" She repeatedly crushed its numerous hard segments with her hiking boot. *Whew, I sure didn't expect that!*

One beautiful day, when Crazy Guy went to town, she felt like taking off her clothes in the trees behind the house while searching among the cow pies for magic mushrooms. A white pueo (owl) with an immense wing-spread started out of the branches. She was in awe of this wonder when she happened upon what she thought were magic mushrooms, so she ate a few. In moments, her stomach started to cramp. As she headed back to the house in a state of nausea, she noticed the German paniolo, standing by his white truck stalking her. She grabbed her clothes and ran inside. She vomited those "magic mushrooms," but not before she locked all the doors. She began to sense that she was in a dangerous situation; she heard a warning in her head to be very careful. Her depth perception was kicking in.

When Crazy Guy returned from town, she heard him yelling from the kitchen, at a rat in the attic. *He **was** crazy, after all.*

"I hear you, King Rat! I know you der! Don't you try come down here!" Crazy Guy ranted. He kept food on the counter since there was no electricity connected to this house to run a refrigerator. Soup, dairy products, bread; everything was on the counter to tempt a rat.

In the next moment, Crazy Guy was yelling at her. "Maya? You der, Maya?"

"Yeah?"

"I got something say you."

"OK. I'll be right there."

"Ron, from the ranch is coming morning, get you."

"The German paniolo? Coming to get me? Why?"

"He taking you back to da ranch."

"What? Forget that! I'm not going!"

"Can't tell one paniolo. He coming morning."

Maya was in full control now. *Bad vibes here! I can split on short notice. Everything I own fits in the pack.* She loaded her backpack and was gone before dawn.

The moonlight and stars shone brightly as she trekked towards the desert side of the gap. *I knew it was too good to be true. I'll never find a place to live on Maui! I absolutely have got to go to Honolulu. I have had enough of this.*

By sun up, she had walked five miles and was very thirsty. "Ah, prickly pears!" *I'll just pull out the spines and take a nice juicy bite.* "Uh, oh! Ouch, didn't see... get out all the spines. They're in my tongue. Oo!" *There's a house and the light is on.*

A woman about her own age answered the door.

"Hello, my name is Maya. Sorry to bother you, but I need some help. I've got prickly pear spines in my tongue!"

"Oh, that's awful. Please, please come in, come in."

"Thanks. I was so thirsty! I thought I got all the spines out, but I was wrong. Ouch! My tongue is burning."

The woman handed her a glass of water and said, "Swish this around real good."

Maya complied and grimaced.

"Let me see." The woman looked closely at Maya's tongue. "The spines are gone now.

It just hurts where the spines were stuck. The pain will subside," she assured her. She refilled the glass with ice water. "Here, swish some cold water around in your mouth. That will seal up the sore spots."

"Thanks." Maya swished some more. Some of the soreness dissipated. "You are so kind. How nice to have another female to talk to. I've been living with Crazy Guy down the road in Kaupo, and a German paniolo is coming after me today. So I split."

"Crazy Guy! Oh no! Wow! Good you got out of there! The first woman wasn't so lucky."

"Really? What happened?"

"She got raped by one of the paniolos."

"Raped! Whoa! Boy, that was what they were going to do to me!"

"You know something? I think I know you. What's your name?"

"Maya is my name. I've never been around here before."

"No, it's not from here that I know you. I think we were in high school together."

"In high school? In California?"

"Yes! What's your real name?"

"It's Jolene Andrews. Maya is my hippie handle."

"I thought so."

"What is your name?"

"I am Sharon Franklin. Do you remember me?"

"I remember a girl named Sharon Franklin. She was really fat."

"Yes, that was me."

"Wow! You look and seem so different."

"My life is different. I have a couple of kids now."

"Wow! What a surprise!" Are you married?"

"Not anymore. He died. But the community helps me out a lot. They bring me food and other stuff that I need for me and the kids."

"Oh, I am sorry to hear that you lost your husband, Sharon. The community helps you? Are you talking about the paniolos, too?"

"Yes. They are very nice to me."

"But...."

"You're a pretty haole girl, all alone. Doesn't work too well here."

"But, what about you?"

"Oh, I'm a mother, and I was married to a local guy."

"Hm. Yes, that is definitely a different story than mine. Well, I better keep going. I've got a long walk ahead of me. Could you spare a bottle of water?"

"Sure. I'll get you one."

"Thanks, again. I'll come by again, if I can ever find a place to settle. But I will probably go back to Honolulu, where I can get a job."

"Well, if you don't leave, please come back and visit me again."

"Sure, and thanks for helping me out."

"Of course."

Maya set out again on the dusty road between Kaupo and Kanaio. She walked many more miles through the desert, thinking all the way.

They honor her and even bring her food. She fits the paniolos' status quo. She does not need to find peace; she lives in serenity. I'll start over again in Honolulu...no place for me here.

As Maya drudged along the dirt road, she saw a sign that said 'Kanaio'. "Hey, Kanaio; that's where that guy Jack "Fingers" lives." *He said he lived by a church. He invited me to stop by.* After a while, Maya spotted a steeple on the hillside. *Well, I guess I'm not in any real hurry.* Maya carefully pushed the brambles aside on the hill as she walked up to the church. When she reached the top, there was a small shack next to the church. She knocked on the door and Jack opened it.

"Beautiful Maya! You made it! Far out, lady! Come on in, come on in."

Jack pulled against the wind to shut the door. Mobiles made of glass and metal pieces hung from his ceiling. As the wind blew through the shack, they clanged like a magnificent orchestra.

Maya was spellbound. "These are wonderful! Did you make them?"

"Yes. And I make kalimbas too."

"What's a kalimba?"

Jack led Maya into an alcove and showed her a small shiny box with gold metal keys. He tapped the keys of the kalimba in time with the mobiles that were now in full swing from the intense airstream blowing through the open windows.

Watching and listening to Jack play, Maya felt the urge to rise and move. "I must dance." She twirled and swayed lightly to the chiming, clinking, and clanking of the mobiles. Absorbed, high on the hill in Kanaio, she floated on the wind.

As the sun set, Maya and Jack settled on a bench at the edge of an incline under the wide open sky. Jack lit a pipe filled with hashish. A sweet taste, a fine aroma, and it was gentle on her lungs, which were sore from smoking weed everyday for three months. Their eyes followed an array of swiftly moving clouds. They saw the shapes of horses, elephants, birds, and mountains in the billows. The swift wind moved the clouds along like a train at high speed, as Jack kept time with his fingers.

Later that evening, coming down from her high, Maya witnessed a ton of cockroaches in Jack's kitchen when she went to get a drink of water. They were crawling everywhere: on the floors, on the table, on the stove, on the window sills and counters. "I let the cockroaches have the kitchen at night," Jack said. Maya was grossed out. *I wonder if he has rats too.*

"Stay here with me," Jack pleaded.

"Thanks, I can't. I need to go to Honolulu and make some money."

"You don't need money here. I'll take care of you."

"Oh, that is a real nice offer, Jack. But I just can't."

Jack "Fingers" was a really special guy, but Maya was not attracted to him or the cockroaches in his kitchen. The next morning, she went on her way again, believing she was edging towards Honolulu and a stable lifestyle.

She stopped in a papaya store in Paia for a snack. The store had all types of papaya products. A group of hikers were buying papaya high energy bars before a trek through Haleakala Crater. A soft-spoken, angelic-looking lady smiled at Maya from behind the counter and said

"You are beautiful, sister." What a sweet thing to say. She had caught Maya's attention.

"If you want to be healthy, sister, all you need is papaya," she stated. "I eat only papaya. It's a complete food. I'm cleansing my body right now by eating only papaya products. My name is Maureen."

"And I am Maya."

Maureen is so kind and positive. "Beautiful, Sister Maya, you must come and visit me! I live in a glass house by a waterfall and stream. I am homesteading. I bathe in the crystal clear water of the stream."

"That sounds nice. It must be very peaceful."

"Oh, it is. And it's magical. Perfect for a beautiful Sister, called Maya."

"Oh, it sounds lovely, but I am on my way back to Honolulu; I haven't been able to find a place to live here."

"Sister, you must come to visit me on my beautiful land before you go." "Sounds wonderful. Far out! I'd sure like to see it." So, Maya postponed her trip to Honolulu. She was feeling free and having fun again.

Maureen's straight papaya cleansing plan was intensive. She got weak and started hemorrhaging and asked Maya to watch her house while she went to the Mainland for medical help. Her small house of glass and screen doors blended into nature. It was beautiful, and so was Maureen. Maya gladly accepted the house-sitting position.

After just a few days on the homestead, Maya noticed a guy hanging out on the land. A fellow with bushy blond uncombed hair parked his VW bus on Maureen's land. He kept staring at Maya through the glass panes; she felt vulnerable. He didn't go away. He just hung around and stared. She was scared of what he might do. For safety's sake, Maya knew she had to leave the "beautiful" situation, where she bathed in the fresh pond and waterfall and ate papaya products all day long. She hoped Maureen would understand when she returned and she wasn't there. She left her a note with an earnest explanation.

So, once more donning her backpack, Maya headed down the road. She hitched a ride to Wailuku. Again, she thought it best to go to

Honolulu. But the driver invited her to a party... a non-stop party. Maya couldn't turn down a party. She was due for some fun. It turned out to be more fun than she needed. Three parties melded into one, lasting all day and night.

The first party was a wedding, officiated by no other than Jack "Fingers," as "Minister" in his refurbished church in Kanaio. People brought tons of flowers to decorate the recessed church windows. The wedding couple was dressed in old-time wedding clothes from a thrift store. The couple recited self-composed vows to each other. Jack nodded and waved his arms in approval during the ceremony; that was his specialty after all. The bride happened to have been Crazy Guy's former girlfriend, the one who was raped by the paniolos. Maya was glad she had gotten away in time, but she felt like she was now going backwards having just visited Jack "Fingers." There was music, food, and hashish. It was a lot of fun and very far out... hard to pull away. But she now had a chronic cough from having smoked so much hashish and marijuana in the previous three months on Maui.

The party traveled to another house and went on to yet another house the next day.

People were beginning to crash. The non-stop celebration was exhausting. Soothsayer-style, a young woman trailed around the party room amid the stoned hippies, repeating, "It's all a cosmic joke." By now, that idea resounded with Maya's experiences; but, she wasn't sure what the girl meant exactly. She requested clarification.

"Are people being manipulated like clown puppets by the Great Powers that be?" Maya asked. "I feel like that at times. I can't seem to break loose."

"It's all a cosmic joke," the girl repeated endlessly, walking in circles around the room. She was making a statement, not a point for discussion. She was like a stuck recording, a wise orator trying to make a point. The idea summed up Maya's sentiments.

Maya was so worn out that she fell asleep at the third party, next to a blasting stereo speaker. Cocaine was being sniffed; fortunately, she slept through it. When she awoke in the morning, the party was headed downhill from the verdant hillsides of Kula to the beach, piled into in an open jeep, moving at full speed. Cramped and scared, she politely asked to be let out of the car. "I feel like walking. It's such a beautiful day."

"It's been far out, sister! We can't believe how you slept by the speaker!"

Maya just smiled and watched the jeep speed off down the mountain.

"Yeah, real far out, man," she sneered soberly, after they've departed. Maya walked through the lush green countryside with the vast ocean down below, in the direction of Wailuki. She took a couple of rides from straight-looking families.

Having had enough of all these crazy places and parties, Maya decided to stay in a hotel that night. She checked into a room above a saloon, the only hotel in Wailuku. By midnight, the saloon was packed with a rowdy crowd; sleeping was impossible. It wasn't just the noise downstairs that bothered her; it was the fist that flew through her door that got her up and out. She opened the door to see two guys having it out in the hall. So again, she packed her stuff and this time sought solace in the arms of Jeff, the owner of the restaurant across the street. She had been in a play skit at his restaurant a few weeks back and had danced at one of his parties.

Resigned, Maya told Jeff, "I'm going to Honolulu. Maui is beautiful, but I don't seem to fit in here and I need to find work."

"You'll find your niche here. Don't give up," Jeff assured her. She wanted to believe him, but she had her doubts. The next day, she was on a plane to Honolulu, where she found a clean apartment, a good job, and a new sense of what it meant to be free.

Earth Dance

"A person who never made a mistake never tried anything new."
~ Albert Einstein

"You must learn from the mistakes of others. You can't possibly live long enough to make them all yourself."
~ Samuel Levenson

"I'd rather be strongly wrong than weakly right."
~ Tallulah Bankhead

Terry and Betty were best friends. Terry was a dancer and had been training since childhood. Betty was talented in many disciplines including dance, music, photography, and painting. Because Betty's perspectives were always unique and inspiring, Terry regarded her as her personal muse.

One Friday, after working very hard in the dance studio, Terry set out with Betty for a relaxing hike to the Lava Cliffs to find a spot to paint the ocean. It seemed like another "Lucky Live Hawaii" day, with a cloudless blue sky, bright sunshine, and a gentle wind. They wove their way in and around the contours of an old lava outcropping on the edge of a swirling ocean in Portlock, a Honolulu suburb, gradually descending to a level spot to paint. Always prepared, Betty had brought all the painting materials in her backpack.

As they painted, they heard the wind whistling around the cliffs and the waves crashing against the rocks below, a symphony of nature that precluded talking.

They hardly noticed the passage of time until the sun began to set. As they realized it was getting dark, they hastily packed up their supplies, preparing to hike back.

Betty started to retrace their steps, but Terry stopped her short. "Which way are you going, Betty?"

"The way we came."

Terry pointed up the side of the lava cliff. "Let's go this way, straight up. I can see the top from here."

"I think we should go around the cliff, the way we came." Terry agreed it was the best way to return, but she was concerned that it was getting dark.

She stubbornly insisted, "That's the long way. Look, the sun is almost down. We don't really have time to go back the way we came and the top is right there. Straight up is the shortest distance."

Terry confidently headed up the steep incline. Betty followed reluctantly.

It was easy at first. The shelves of lava they used as hand and foot holds at the bottom of the mountain were wide, thick, and sturdy. But as they ascended, the shelves gradually grew narrow, shallow, and brittle.

"It's still not too late to descend and go back around the long way," Betty suggested.

"Maybe if we had flashlights…but we don't and, look, the sun is about gone now. It isn't that much farther to the top," Terry replied. Betty shook her head and kept following Terry as she ascended the receding cliff.

When they looked down now, the level area was far away. The comforting warm plateau on which they had painted looked menacing, as if it could crack a skull. And the waves, rendered almost inaudible by the distance, thrashed hungrily below.

In the faded light, the shallow lava outcroppings began to crumble as they touched them. Terry was no longer confident she'd made the right decision, but it was too late, too far, and too dangerous to go back and walk around the cliff as Betty had suggested. Terry's heart raced. As she looked at Betty, she trembled and tears rolled down her cheeks.

"I've never seen you like this, Terry."

Betty seemed to be in perfect control. Terry began exhaling deeply to calm herself, but she couldn't stop crying. "I don't want to die, Betty."

"What? Terry, I've never seen you like this. I'm surprised at you."

"Betty, I want to live; I want to dance!"

"Then dance, dance now. Get up in second position on your knees; dig your knees into the sand. Don't panic; dance with the Earth; it will support you."

Terry did as Betty instructed her to do even though she was frightened, feeling herself sliding with the crumbling lava. Breathing deeply to calm herself, she dug her knees into the sand and reached towards the next fragile outcropping.

"Lift yourself up. Don't put any pressure on the lava; touch it lightly and keep moving up. Walk on your knees," Betty commanded.

I am not sure I can make it to the top; but Betty believes I have it in me – that I know how to do this 'Earth Dance'.

How did this happen? How did I get in this predicament? She really couldn't stop to answer that question right then.

Betty disappeared every once in a while and then returned, still carrying their backpacks. She was actually walking. *This woman is superhuman!* Betty was perfectly at ease, balanced and walking upright with their backpacks, from location to location.

Terry was able to keep cool until the hand holds, the shallow ledges, were not only brittle but far apart. "I can't reach the next one, Betty." Again, she began to tremble and gasp.

"Do a cartwheel," Betty ordered.

"What? That's impossible! I can't do that!"

"It is possible. You can do it; you've done it in dance class many times."

"But that was on level ground."

"Do it! Do it, now!"

Terry did a cartwheel. By some miraculous means, she balanced on her hands and flipped her legs and feet gently onto the next fragile piece of lava. No pressure, it was like walking on air. From there, the top was but a scramble away. *I did it, I did it.* "I did it, Betty, I did it!"

"Of course, you did it. I knew you could do it."

"What a friend you are, Betty. I don't know what I'd do without you. You saved my life."

"You're the one who did the dance."

It was dark when they reached the top, but they were safe.

"Betty, you were right from the beginning when you suggested that we go back the way we came."

"It was the logical thing to do."

"I guess I'm not too logical."

"Don't worry about it. We're back now."

"Yeah, but, can you tell me one thing?'

"Sure, what?"

"How did you just walk up that cliff? And you carried the backpacks too!"

"I just knew how to do it. I had Outward Bound training. I kept moving and leaned into the mountain."

"I wish I had your know-how."

"Believe in yourself more, Terry. You're the one who did the dance. You can do a lot of stuff."

"Yeah, I guess so. But it sure helps to have friends who can choreograph like you. You always amaze me."

"It is always a pleasure to spend time with you."

"Really. Even today?"

"Especially today."

Like Clara, the "It Girl"

"They were smart and sophisticated, with an air of independence about them, and so casual about their looks and clothes and manners as to be almost slapdash. I don't know if I realized as soon as I began seeing them that they represented the wave of the future, but I do know I was drawn to them. I shared their restlessness, understood their determination to free themselves of the Victorian shackles of the pre-World War I era and find out for themselves what life was all about."
~ Colleen Moore, Actress

In 1927, at age sixteen, bouncy little Sarah Schwartz got a part dancing and singing in the musical *The Girl Friend* at the theatre in the Jewish Community Center in Baltimore. She loved to sing and dance. She had learned and honed her skills by copying performers in films shown at the local movie theatre and practicing with her friends. She never did that kind of thing at home, and she never told her parents about getting the part. They wouldn't have approved. Her parents were from the old school, having come over on the boat from Russia in the latter part of the nineteenth century. Her father, Hyman, was strict. He adhered to the belief that "children should be seen and not heard." To him, Sarah was still a child, not a budding young woman who needed to express herself. He prided himself in keeping his seven children in line, but Sarah, her sister Polly, and her brothers were ready to flee the coop at the first opportunity.

On the second day of the show, Hyman, a small man, was having pastrami on rye with his buddy, Sid, a large man with a paunch straining the buttons of his vest, was indulging in a piece of cherry cheesecake, in the Jewish Community Center snack bar. Except for a face hardened by struggling to raise a family in the new country on the meager income of a produce peddler with a horse drawn carriage, Hyman resembled a thin little boy lost in his pin-striped suit. Having been undernourished while growing up in Russia, he was only five feet tall, and was doing his best to make a better life for his wife and seven children in America.

"Ho, ho, Hyman, you're a big man... an actress daughter."

"Me big? Ha, ha! You're the one who is big and getting bigger with that cake! Vat, Sid? Vat is that you said? Mine daughter is a young kid, no actress. You must be mistaken."

"Ho no, Hyman. She's here now, singing and dancing on the stage, in the theater."

"Sid, you're nuts! She's home, cleaning the house, making cheese blintzes with her mother," Hyman replied, taking a bite of his thick sandwich and dismissing Sid's comment by waving his arm in the air.

"You're calling me a liar? Vould I lie to a friend?"

"I certainly hope not!" Hyman leaned closer to the table and looked intently at Sid. Taking a sharp bite of his pastrami sandwich, Hyman slammed the table with his left hand.

"Scuse me! I should lie? Then go see with your own eyes. She is wowing them with her cute little dance and flirty girty smile."

"'Cute little dance? Flirty girty smile? NO! Can't be! I won't allow it."

With a piece of pastrami and mustard hanging from his long beard, Hyman threw back his chair and stalked out of the snack bar. "I von't allow it!" he roared.

When Hyman swung open the theatre door, the usher tried to hold him back. But Hyman went full steam ahead – there was no stopping him. He didn't need a seat, for as far as he was concerned, the show was over. He spotted her, his own daughter Sarah, on the stage in a fringed short dress, wearing lots of makeup, and shaking her hips as she sang.

"Oy gevalt!" Hyman yelled. "Stop that right now, right this minute!" Hyman waved his hairy arms in the air and lowered his head, like a ram about to attack, and darted forward. "Mine daughter doesn't do this!" he shouted as he reached the stage. "I von't allow it! Stop this show! Sarah, you come here right now." Hyman walked right up on to the stage and grabbed his stunned daughter by the arm, yanking her down the steps, up the aisle, and out the door. In the foyer, he scolded, "I forbid you to make a spectacle of yourself, to embarrass your family like this."

"But...."

"No but," he said as he dragged her home. "No buts about it."

Sarah had numerous "buts," but she couldn't voice them, knowing her father could be violent. He didn't spare the strap when it came to disobedient children.

Sarah was furious – it was time to venture out into the world. *He won't do that to me again! That's it! I'm leaving.* Shortly thereafter, she quit school and went to Chicago to party with her red-headed cousin Reba, who knew all the good places to dance. She sparked to the music and rhythms of the big city. Like the song, she was "five foot two" and "oh what those five feet can do." "Flapper, flapper, yes one of those." "Turned up nose, rolled down hose." She mastered the Charleston, the Lindy Hop, bobbed her hair, and returned to Baltimore, a woman of her time. She got a job in Herschel Cohn's, selling stylish women's dresses, and shared a flat with her friend Mabel, who also loved to dance.

It was the roaring twenties. No one was more ready for the excitement of the era than Sarah and Mabel. They were just like their screen idol Clara Bow, the epitome of flaming youth in rebellion. "We're 'It Girls' like Clara Bow," Mabel observed with a giggle when they went to see the movie of the same title. There was no mistaking this fact – they were flirtatious, bubbly, and outrageous, just like the "It Girl" in the movie.

"Catch this, Mabel," Sarah read from the newspaper. "Here's a picture of Clara Bow using a pair of scissors to lower the neckline of her dress. Do we have a scissors?"

"You bet!"

They chopped away the upper third of their best dresses. Trying on her altered dress with the plunged neckline, Sarah exclaimed, "Just call me Clara."

"Clara, wow! You look just like her, with the bob and all. Your father would have a fit if he saw you."

"He won't. He'll never find out. Now, let's get ready for the dance... and meeting that special someone."

"Sounds good to me. Just call me Greta... as in Garbo."

"Hi ya, Greta!"

At the ballroom dance, vivacious Clara, in her new red dress, noticed a fancy-stepping man on the dance floor. He was tall, dark, and handsome. Turning to her friend, now wearing a blond wig, Clara said, "Look at that one, Greta, that good lookin' fella can really swing."

"Yeah, that one would be a good catch," Greta agreed. "As for me, "I vant to be alone.""

"Suit yourself, doll. I'm after that one."

Clara smiled and flashed her eyes at the striking fellow as he twirled his partner and smiled in her direction. He caught her drift and gave her the high sign. When the music stopped, he positioned himself near her and they beamed at each other. Clara didn't budge an inch when he sat right down next to her, even though there was barely enough room to breathe.

He whispered into her ear, "My name is Fred and I like red." His eyes sparkled. Clara melted.

"My name is Clara, and I like you," Clara hummed, as she gazed into his eyes.

"Boogie woogie, Baby?" Fred asked as he stood up, bowed, and extended his hand.

Clara laughed and accepted, "Oh, yeah! You've got it, kid. See you later, Greta, darling."

Greta waved her off. She knew it would be a whole lot later.

Fred swirled Clara onto the dance floor.

Simultaneously smitten, Fred and Clara danced the night away.

Little did Clara know that Fred had an overly protective mother.

"And where have you been, young man?" demanded Fred's mother, Fran, the next morning when he returned home at breakfast time. She was a small woman with a dark complexion, frizzy brown hair, and a sharp tongue. Leaning forward across the table, she waited for his answer. "Huh?" She sipped her coffee and tapped her foot impatiently on the linoleum.

Fred didn't like it when she stared him down like that. Finally, he told her, "I went to the dance at the Lord Baltimore."

"Dance? You were dancing until 8 o'clock in the morning?"

"Well, not exactly. I had an early breakfast with friends."

"Friends, huh?"

A pattern developed. Fred continued to come home late, hoping to avoid his mother's glare. But she knew – she didn't fall asleep until he got in.

"So?" she said one day, after a week of this new habit of his sneaking in before daylight. "So?" She waited for his explanation.

"So what?"

"What! What do you mean 'what'? Enough of 'what'! That's what! You have your nerve coming home every morning before the rooster crows! Have you been with a woman? Tell me the truth!"

"Gee, Mom, gimme a break!"

"Break! You want a break? I'll give you! Out with it! You can't hide things from your mother."

"I'm a grown man! I'm not hiding anything."

"Huh! That's what you think!"

"Look, I've met a real nice gal. She loves to dance. She's real good."

"A nice gal, huh? A real good gal, huh? An all night gal? What's nice about that? She's a flapper. That's not the kind of woman for my son. That's the end of that. I want you home before midnight. Do you hear?" She placed her folded hands firmly on her lap.

"She's a swell gal, Mom."

"'Swell', huh! We'll see how 'swell'."

Instead of going dancing that night, Fred and Clara eloped. Fran had no choice in the matter. Fred had a little savings and a steady job.

Even after Fred and Clara were married and in their own home and had two children, Fran was still trying to "free" her son from "that flapper." That made it difficult for Clara to be her ebullient self. Fran regularly admonished Clara in front of Fred and the children.

"Control yourself," she'd say to Clara when she felt she was too loud. "Act like a respectable woman, someone my son can be proud of."

"I don't have to take that! Where do you get off talking to me like that?"

It was moments like this that provoked the old rebel in Clara. She visited with her friend Greta for coffee to discuss old times and to vent her frustration.

"He isn't like he was when I first met him, Greta. And I never knew that he was tied to his mother's apron strings! If I don't get him away from her, I'll never have any fun again. And she is turning my kids against me. I need to find a way out. My father was bad enough, now I've got a bossy mother-in-law."

"You don't need that, Clara!"

"I've got an idea. You know my sister Polly?"

"Yeah, the one who went to Las Vegas?"

"That's the one. She is a smart cookie. My brothers got a letter from Polly inviting them to move out west to make a fortune selling ice cream in the desert."

"Yeah? So?"

"I'm gonna go, too. Can you think of anything more exciting?"

"Oh, but Clara I would miss you. I know we haven't seen each other much the last couple of years, but I really hate to see you leave for good."

"Nothing to stop you from coming out for a visit," Clara said.

"Well, nothing except time and money, I guess. Well, don't let me stop you. You're going to have a great time out west. But what about Fred? Will he go?"

"He'll have to go if he wants to stay with me and the kids. I'm not changing my mind."

Fred was resistant.

"My family is here!" Fred exclaimed.

"So? Big deal! I'm going! Are you coming?"

Clara packed up the car in one day and let a realtor handle the house sale.

Just like that. Fred didn't like ultimatums. He gave in for the sake of harmony and the kids.

Of course, his mother put up a fight, but she was no match for Clara. "You're going to leave your mother and father and brothers for a flapper?" Fran asked.

"She's my wife and she's taking the kids. I have to go," Fred answered.

"Oy vey! I knew this would happen. A mother always knows best. Don't forget your home, where you are from. You can always come back. Las Vegas is a bad town. Lots of crime. No place for a nice boy like you," Fran cried. Fred gave his mother a pat on the back and a quick hug.

"I have to go, Mom. Clara is waiting in the car. Good bye, Mom."

"Wait." Too late. Fred was out the door.

* * *

After only one year in Las Vegas, it was obvious that "mother knew best" as far as Fred was concerned. A nice boy like Fred didn't belong in the City of Sin. He couldn't fight his temptation to gamble.

When Fred came home without a paycheck, Clara asked, "Where did the money go?"

"I placed it on Assault, the Triple Crown Winner."

"A horse? What? You bet our mortgage money on a horse?"

"Yes, the horse… he was supposed to place first. He always does."

"And? What then? This time he didn't. You fool."

"He lost. What can I say?"

"You've said it! You placed your whole paycheck on a horse? And he lost? You jerk!"

"I told you we shouldn't have come out west. Everyone back east warned us."

"Everyone? Like your mother, you mean?"

"Mother did say that Las Vegas had a bad reputation. She read in the newspaper that lots of people fell into gambling in Las Vegas."

"Fell in, huh? Reputation? Sounds like your Mother all right! All she ever thinks about is 'reputation.' Even I didn't have the reputation that was good enough for her son, did I? You spent and lost our mortgage payment. Where's your backbone?"

"Don't get so upset. He was supposed to win. He was the favored horse."

"But, he didn't win, did he? Mama's boy, mama's boy! That's what you are. Nobody forced you to lose our money like that, Mama's boy. Why don't you just go home to Mama?"

* * *

So Fred took Clara's advice. He returned to Baltimore. He met a nice quiet girl, the kind that Fran approved off. They married and settled down to raise a new family.

* * *

Clara, fiercely independent, made a point of not living in the past and moved forward with determination; she was forever the "It Girl."

Déjà Vu

*"Do I Believe in Computer Dating? Only If the
Computers Really Love Each Other."*
~Groucho Marx

His picture on the seniors' dating website appealed to me. He was tall, slim, blond, fit, and had a charming smile. He lived in Albuquerque, New Mexico. I lived in Las Vegas, Nevada. He was far away, but his looks and profile appealed to me. He had a Masters' degree like me, and was an avid reader. An educated, good-looking man... worth a shot. He did look a lot like Bill, an old boyfriend. But, of course, he wasn't Bill; I didn't want him to be Bill. In fact, I didn't want anything to do with him if he was like Bill. What happened 30 years ago didn't warrant an encore.

Next step: send him an email. "Hello, I am interested in getting to know you. Hope distance won't be an issue." I wasn't in a hurry. I figured we would be able to get to know each other slowly over the web, and if we seemed compatible, one of us could travel for an in-person meeting.

I was overjoyed when I received a reply. He said, "Hello. My name is Edward. Call or email me." That was followed by his phone number and a personal email address. I wasn't ready to do that!

I replied, "I wish to email through the service and take time getting to know you before doing that."

I was relieved by his response, "Going slow is fine – and a good idea in this day and age." Further, he commented that if asked, he would advise his granddaughter to do just that. That made me feel safe; he couldn't possibly be like Bill. He sounded like an even-tempered gentleman. *Yippie!*

We communicated daily by email through the dating site. I looked forward to reading his messages every day; he was eloquent and always had something interesting to say. I learned more about him. He was originally from the Midwest and was raised on a farm.

I jokingly commented, "Ah, you are of farm stock."

He readily added, "My doctor told me I was quite strong and healthy, that physically, I am 20 years younger than my chronological age of 70." I was impressed. He had 2 grown, married children, and 6 beautiful and talented grand-children. He said he worked hard as an engineer from May until September and traveled the rest of the year.

Is fate shining on me?

We expanded our online conversation with in-depth discussions about books, romance, religion, philosophy, travel, and extrasensory perception. We'd both had had ESP experiences. He told me, "I recall seeing my Mother after she died. It was as if she was actually there, talking to me. I think many things that happen in our lives are influenced by unseen spiritual forces," he added. "I have had a few brief experiences like this."

"I have had experiences like that too," I replied. "Once I created a snake-charming go-go dancer character in a play that I was writing, who later manifested in my life. When I am in a very relaxed state, I regularly receive messages about what to write and about other things. I always keep a writing pad nearby."

He remarked, "You are more advanced than I am."

"Maybe only in ESP, but certainly not in some of the areas in which you excel."

After about 2 weeks of favorable emails, my new found friend, Edward, was ready for a visit, but I wasn't. So, we continued our email exchanges and added phone calls, which appeared to deepen our rapport. In one of the books we both read and discussed, the author stated, "Fate doesn't make house calls." Edward liked that one and interpreted is as follows: "You have to go after what you want in life."

I'd never thought about fate in that regard, especially if it was about a relationship with a man. I retained the idea, fantasy or not, that it is fate that brings people together or pulls them apart. Not really a controlled thing, from my point of view. I liked looking for signs which came to me intuitively. *I am not into chasing things down.*

Valentine's Day was coming up and I visualized a special time with my "new man." I was ready for that wonderful in-person first meeting. At the beginning of that week, he informed me that he was going to Nebraska to visit his daughter and to see his granddaughter perform in a play on Valentine's Day. Well, what could I say... nothing, really. I thought the next opportunity wouldn't be far off in the distance. I knew he was planning a trip to Ecuador about a week and a half later, but I was hoping he would come for a visit before he left. But that didn't happen. Of course, I accepted he had a lot to do to prepare for a trip like that. He said he would come for a visit after he returned. He added, "It might be difficult to contact you by internet and phone calls, but I will try to contact you at least once during my trip to Ecuador." I didn't hear anything from Edward during his two weeks in South America.

From then on the calls and emails trickled to almost nothing. I began to lose hope that I'd ever meet him. He did call when he returned from Ecuador, but said he had to postpone his trip to Las Vegas to meet me due to illness and a work project.

When I heard from him again about a week later, he said he was coming in another week, much to my surprise. He changed the date a few times; he always had a good reason, but the reasons seemed to conflict with each other. By then, I figured he'd met someone closer to home and traveled with or met a lady in Ecuador. But I hung onto to the hope that he would show up sometime.

To my surprise, he actually made a reservation and arrived in Las Vegas a couple of weeks later. I had only heard from him about 3 times in the last month, so I was skeptical and cautious.

We met at an upscale Italian restaurant. Edward was out in front, when I drove up. He looked good, even better than his picture. I'd been watching my diet and exercising a lot. I looked good too and felt great. There was still possibility here, I thought....

He met me at my car door, as I parked. "May I give you a kiss... a hug?"

"You'd better give me a hug," I replied. He hugged me warmly. We were pleased with each other.

Once we were seated in the restaurant, a surreal sequence of events began to occur. We were at a small square table; I was sitting on the right side of Edward, which gave me a side view of him. "I like the way you look," he smiled and I smiled back. As we were looking at our menus, I sensed something and glanced at his back. That is when I saw armor-like hackles spring out about 6 inches from his lower back, recoil, and then reverberate up his spine. This was followed by his right shoulder shooting up and down like a plunger. I couldn't believe my eyes. The shoulder continued to spasm in the same manner then, and on and off during the two days that I was around him. It was very odd, but I didn't feel that I knew him well enough to discuss it or tell him about the odd thing which I had perceived. I didn't want to be judgmental or picky. I rationalized to myself that "no one was perfect." I wanted it to be perfect... but I was concerned. He had mentioned previously that he didn't have or need health insurance. Something didn't make sense. He obviously had some kind of a condition.

We had a pleasant lunch, followed by a lively walk in a neighborhood desert park and tasty peanut butter frozen yogurts. But I became irritated by a habit he had of tapping me and slapping me on the shoulder when he talked to me. I began having a feeling of déjà vu; I asked him if he too was having a déjà vu feeling. He said no. Being with him reminded me again of Bill. *Bill was a tapper, a slapper, and a pusher. Bill was violent!* I asked him to stop the tapping and slapping. "It doesn't hurt, but I find it surprising and distracting."

"I'm sorry. I tend to do that. I won't do it again," he agreed amicably. We made plans for the evening and when I dropped him off at his hotel, he smiled sweetly at me.

* * *

While relaxing at home, I thought about his boyish appeal. I dismissed the associations with Bill and instead imagined that he was really like Kenny, my first love and perhaps only true love. I ran with that idea and was filled with a sense of lightness. At times, how easily one can delude oneself. I wanted him to be the ONE; I wanted it to be perfect. Then I remembered that Bill had a charming facade. I wanted the impossible.

We had dinner at a small Korean/Japanese restaurant which I frequented often for its quaint environment, good food, and "free sake after 6." We were both elated from the fun we'd had earlier that day and the possibilities that lay ahead. We laughed a lot and I told him about a discussion a writer friend and I had had in this very restaurant, at the very same table, a week earlier. I related to him, "My friend is writing a biography about her mother and growing up in the Midwest. She said that people there were 'nice but not necessarily good.' I told her that would make a great title for the biography or for a chapter in her book."

Edward readily agreed, "Nice but not necessarily good. Yes, that's true and a good title. My Midwest Norwegian family sweep unpleasant things under the rug to keep appearances pleasant."

Everything was nice, nice, nice, and of course, pleasant with us, except for this gnawing suspicion that tried to claim my attention that this guy was a lot like Bill, charming, but dangerous. My ESP antenna was on alert. But I was also trying to sweep my distrust under the rug.

After dinner, we parked in the covered garage at his hotel to go see a comedy show. When we got out of the car, I wrapped my arm in his. Gallantly, he took my arm, like a prince joining a royal procession…

and he squeezed it tightly... too tightly. I tried to loosen it, but when I stopped moving, he had my wrist in a vice and held it there. I ask him to loosen up but he didn't. I kept trying to free my wrist to no avail, he gripped it even tighter... and I didn't feel that I knew him well enough to make a big deal out of it, and didn't want to ruin the evening, the wonderful day. I continued in my delusion of everything being nice and even good.

During the show, he seemed very cold. He didn't put his arm around me or reach for my hand. We enjoyed the show and laughed a lot. In the parking lot, at my car, he embraced me for a kiss and I refused, saying, "It would be too distracting." I was feeling turned on, but also cautious; we still had another day together. I hadn't liked the way he gripped my arm, tapped and slapped me on the shoulder, and I still felt uneasy about the weird back thing I'd observed at lunch in the Italian restaurant.

The next day, we were to meet at the Springs Preserve café for lunch and a walk through the gardens. He arrived late and in a huff. "I got caught in a traffic jam. There was an accident." By the way he was acting, all strung out, you'd think the accident had happened to him. His usual nice demeanor and smile were absent; instead, he wore a scowl and the pigment on his face had dark splotches. In fact, he looked and acted like a different person. He seemed inordinately upset for just being delayed in traffic. We bought some sandwiches at the café and took our lunch to a sunlit place in the children's play area of the Preserve. We smiled and commented on the children playing and everything seemed ok, for a while. But then, as we walked, an undertone of bickering arose. We both seemed to be short on patience. Upon noticing a plant, he kept questioning, "What is that plant? It looks like one that grows outside where I live, but that is a tree. The one by my house is more like a bush, low to the ground."

I finally said, "You'll know soon when we get to the tour garden. It has signs identifying all the plants."

He questioned again, as if he hadn't heard me. I kept repeating myself, as well, sharper each time. When we got to the gardens, his question was answered when he read the sign by the plant, but his impatience grew. It was palatable. The points on his back from yesterday seemed to surround us with jabs.

* * *

After leaving the Preserve, we went to the YMCA for a workout. The desk attendant gave us a couple of towels.

"Give me my towel," he demanded.

He acted like I was keeping the towel, instead of just holding it for him. Afterward, changing in the men's room, he didn't greet or join me in the gym. I was on the stationary bike. Without looking for me, he stepped on and started up a treadmill. I went over to him to tell him, "I will be doing some sit ups in the back with the trainer." Later, the trainer walked with me to Edward's treadmill. "This is Milton, my trainer. This is my friend, Edward." Edward smiled broadly at the trainer, even stopped running for a few minutes to converse with him. They laughed loudly as they discussed football.

After the workout, before getting in our cars, we talked about the evening plans. For some reason, I mentioned that the author of the book we both read contradicted himself about the question of fate in the story. With a dark and gloomy distant look, he replied, "That's ok. I contradict myself too." He sure had; he wasn't the same warm person I'd been emailing, talking to on the phone, or spending the previous day with. He seemed miles away. *Was fate making a house call, after all? Was he Bill's energy reincarnate? I don't need or want to attract violent energy!*

That evening, we changed plans numerous times, but ended up at a movie chosen by him, about a broken love affair. My leg hurt from overdoing it in the workout, so I asked him to drive. He drove like a maniac. Edward, the reserved gentleman was nowhere to be found. *He has that glint in his eyes. Bill had the same glint in his eyes when he tried to push me down the hill.* "You are doing 80 miles an hour on a city street."

"Oh, I thought this was a highway. There aren't too many cars on the road."

"It's not! On any Nevada road, including highways, 80 miles per hour is considered speeding."

As in the comedy show, he did not attempt to hold my hand or put his arm around me at the movie theater. The seats had a bar between them which lifted up. At one point, well into the movie, I lifted it and took his hand. His body felt rigid next to mine and his hand was stiff. His skin was abrasive like the material on his jacket, which was made from a coarsely-finished animal hide. He held my hand tightly... too tightly. I took his hand in both my hands and stroked it, hoping to relax him. He quickly and roughly rubbed the back of my hand. A vision of Bill holding me down with his arm braced across my neck flashed in my mind. Not good! I was shaking. *This man frightens me.* He was like Bill; there was no denying it. I could feel violent energy surging.

When we got back to the parking lot at the hotel, we looked at each other. I just wanted to get away from him. He buckled his lips to assure me that he wouldn't kiss me, gave me a hug and said nicely, "We'll be in touch." I shook my head. I got in my car and soon I was safely home. No repeat performance needed.

The Almond Cookie

"As you get older three things happen. The first is your memory goes, and I can't remember the other two."
~Sir Norman Wisdom, English Actor, Comedian, and Singer-Songwriter

One day, 70-year-old Pamela visited Chinatown for the first time in twenty years on a mission to purchase a delicious almond cookie. In her youth, she had a tendency to free-associate and wander, adoring the spontaneous, unconstrained association of ideas, emotions, and movement. That behavior, habit, method had worked well for her in the past, but the present was another story. She got lost.

As she drove into the parking garage, she remembered exactly how the almond cookie appeared, felt, and tasted. *The top of the cookie had a golden shiny glaze and right in the middle of it was a sleek almond. The cookie was about 3 inches wide and had a crunchy texture that crumbled when I bit into it before dissolving into a sweet combination of almond and sugar. Surely, they still have them. Every restaurant and bakery in Chinatown served or sold them.* Her mouth watered in anticipation. A lot can change in twenty years, but for Pamela, almond cookies and Chinatown were synonymous.

After parking her car on the second level of the garage, she rode the elevator down to the street exit. The parking structure was not obvious from the street when she got out of the elevator; only shops were visible… but Pamela didn't notice that.

After Pamela walked for a bit, she spotted The Golden Dragon Restaurant with an ornate red and gold entrance that was classy-looking and inviting. *Just like being in China,* Pamela thought. When she was seated, a young Chinese girl appeared to take her order.

"I take your order now."

Pamela didn't even look at the menu. She immediately ordered her old favorite. "I would like a bowl of wonton mein." The soup came and it was delicious. Pamela didn't finish it, however; she wanted to save room for her almond cookie.

The waitress brought her the check and a fortune cookie.

Pamela was quick to add: "Oh, I would like some green tea and one almond cookie, please."

"Sorry, no almond cookie."

How could they not have an almond cookie? I am in a Chinese restaurant in Chinatown. "No almond cookie? How can that be? I always have an almond cookie when I come to Chinatown."

"No more. Choose something else?" The waitress pointed to the bakery case at the front by the cash register. "Black Bean cake?"

"No, thank you. I came to Chinatown for an almond cookie."

"No, no, no almond cookie."

"Okay, just tea then."

After finishing her tea and paying her bill, frustrated but still determined, Pamela foraged through the streets of Chinatown, which were dotted with bakeries. She was sure her desired treat must exist in all of them. "I would like an almond cookie," she asked at the first one which was a block from the restaurant where she had lunch.

"Almond cookie. On shelf in window." On the shelf in the window was a bag of dark-colored small cookies. Not the ticket.

"Oh, no, I just want one big almond cookie. Thank you, anyway."

Imagining she was nibbling, crunching her favored cookie, Pamela walked another block and around another corner to a new bakery. She scanned the display of pastries. Not a single almond cookie was in there, large or small.

By now, she had wandered through the better part of Chinatown. It was hot and humid and her toes were blistered from rubbing against her leather sandals. The pavement, still cobbled from an earlier era, was pitted by wear, causing her to twist her ankles. Derelicts crept out of alleyways. She drew back in fear; but, she trudged on in search of her cookie.

In a very small bakery, she once again asked, "Do you have any almond cookies?" She received an affirmative nod. Her heart beat rapidly, in anticipation. A cookie *almost like* the one she yearned for was held before her.

"Just came out of the oven."

Pamela could smell the cookie's sweetness. "The most important part is missing," she cried out. Where's the almond that goes in the middle?"

The baker agreed, "Almond cookie; no almond."

"But that doesn't make sense; I always used to…"

"One dollar."

"OK." Pamela accepted the less-than-perfect cookie and exited the bakery. No almond, but when she bit into it, the texture, the sweetness was just as she remembered. Twenty years had passed and only one bakery had a semblance of her cookie, but it would have to do.

Pamela stopped at a few more stores to buy some earrings and look at antiques. She had been walking quite a while and was hungry again so she stopped for some dim sum that caught her eye in a window. When she came out of the restaurant, she realized she had lost her bearings, and had no idea which way to walk to find her car. So she just walked with blistered feet by sprawled derelicts, trusting her instincts would lead her to the parking garage. After a while, she recognized some of the same buildings, like The Golden Dragon Restaurant. She was sure she must be close; but, she was just walking in circles and the parking garage was nowhere in sight.

Finally, she spotted a garage. "Ah, the parking lot, at last." She got in an elevator, but it didn't go up to the second floor, only down to a basement office. None of this looked familiar, so she went back to the first floor and stumbled back out to the sidewalk. Then she noticed a sign with arrows pointing in the direction of the police station. But when she followed the arrows, they didn't lead her there. She was even more lost, and by now more hot and tired and sore.

"Where is the police station?" she asked a Chinese woman, who didn't speak English. The woman smiled and kept walking. Desperate, she kept asking, until a gentleman understood her and walked her to the door of the station. The Good Samaritan nodded, smiled, and walked on.

"May I help you, Madame?" the officer in the station asked.

"I can't find my car. I can't even find the parking garage where I parked my car on the second floor."

"What street were you on when you entered the garage?"

"Oh, I do remember that. It was Smith Street."

"OK, look here. I will draw you a map to get there. Go down to the next block, this way, and turn right. You'll find the parking garage there."

"Thank you. I really appreciate it after all I've been through."

"Did somebody rob you?"

"Oh, no, nothing like that."

"What happened then?"

"I couldn't find my almond cookie."

"Almond cookie?"

"Yes, the kind I had in Chinatown 20 years ago."

"Oh. I see. Um… I was just a little kid then. I wouldn't know."

"Yes, oh well. Of course, times change. Thank you. Goodbye, young man."

Time Lapse

"Wisdom doesn't necessarily come with age.
Sometimes age just shows up all by itself."
~Tom Wilson

"Don't let aging get you down. It's too hard to get back up."
~John Wagner

Lucy is lounging by the pool at her desert retirement community. In the midst of a daydream, she sees herself dancing in the waves at Santa Monica Beach, just as she did when she was a teenager growing up in L.A. *I'm going to go do it, going to dive into the ocean and play in the waves.*

When she tells Rita, in the chaise next to her, about her trip, Rita recoils. "Are you nuts? You're 75 years old! Are you really going to drive 600 miles, roundtrip, to frolic in the ocean? People our age just don't *do* that sort of thing. Act your age. Don't go looking for trouble."

"Trouble? I'm not looking for trouble, just some fun."

"Trouble."

"What kind of trouble?"

"Lucy, in case you haven't noticed, we don't have the balance we used to have. Those waves could knock you down and drag you out to sea. You could drown!"

"Oh, come on. My balance isn't perfect but I know how to swim."

"What's wrong with the pool?"

"Well, nothing is wrong with the pool, except maybe the chlorine."

"It is a saline pool."

"With chlorine."

"The ocean has a lot of junk in it, too. Think long slimy kelp wrapping around your legs."

"Oh, I never minded the kelp. I really miss the ocean. Ah, the rise and fall of the waves, the sound of them breaking on the shore."

"Suit yourself. But, don't say I didn't warn you."

Following her dream, Lucy travels to Santa Monica and checks herself into a hotel that's advertised as on the beach, but she's surprised to discover it's across the street from the sand. In between the sand and the hotel is a noisy road with bumper-to-bumper traffic, engine exhaust, crowds, sirens, derelicts, and rotten smells. Once she is settled in her room, she dons her bathing suit and heads for the beach. Determined to enjoy the ocean, she crosses the busy street and moves quickly across the pavement, cluttered with street people. Then, she must hike on the sand for a quarter of a mile to reach the water, but her legs are still strong so she doesn't really mind trudging through sand. It's just not the scene she remembers from childhood.

Lucy arrives at the water's edge. She removes her tie dyed sarong and drops onto the sand to study the tide. Some distance out, brown waves break sharply, spurting out a blanket of foam that gushes towards the shore. Her long white hair blows in the breeze as she watches the young and hardy brave the rapid, hard-breaking waves that slap at their backs and the young children as they skip and leap in the foam.

"…lose your balance…knocked down….dragged out…" She can hear Rita's warnings clearly in her mind and has second thoughts about walking into the churning waves. But she is determined to at least join the less adventurous who wade in the surf. Neatly, she wraps her clothing in the hotel towel and saunters into the water. But the undertow is strong and she must keep an eye on her belongings. People on the beach and in the water all appear to be having a great time, but Lucy is apprehensive about the rough ocean current, the mass of people, and a possible theft of her belongings. Disappointed, she paces back and forth in the area in front of her towel until she grows bored and decides to leave. *So much for happy memories!* Finding a stretch of sidewalk across the sand, she falls into a long line of people plodding toward the pier. Yes, I am seventy-five and this isn't how I remember it all. Her eyes light up when she spots a familiar structure. It's the Hippodrome! As she draws closer, she can hear the carousel organ playing tunes she recalls from long ago. *Could the old Merry-Go-Round still be here? I must have a look.* Breaking from the crowd, she makes her way to the whirling carousel of brightly colored horses. Fascinated, she gazes at the glittering menagerie racing by. Round and round it goes. *This part is just as I remember it…glorious, enchanting. I must have a ride!*

"Only $2 for adults?"

"Yes," the seller smiles.

"I think I was on this Merry-Go-Round when I was a child, in the 40s. How long has it been here?"

"Since 1947."

"Oh-h-h-h! I must go on it again."

Glowing with childlike excitement, Lucy digs in her purse for the two bills and lays them flat on the counter.

When the carousel stops and a new ride begins, Lucy dashes forth to find the perfect horse. No two are alike. They all seem to be in motion, skillfully carved in prancing and leaping poses with regal adornment. Lucy is drawn to a spirited chocolate brown steed with keen eyes, beautifully decked out in a red saddle, golden tassels, and a brocade tapestry breastplate. As she climbs onto his saddle, he appears to be grinning back at her with his mouth agape, a lock of hair on his forehead and his mane curling around his neck. *I'd better strap myself in—this is going to be some ride!* Tingling with anticipation, she gives the horse a slap on the haunch and yells, "Giddy up, Horsey! Let's go!" The brown stallion slowly slides up and down his golden spiral column, as the carousel circles slowly in time to the music. Lucy spies the stenciled rose bushes on the inside of the canopy. *I remember those! How neat! They're still here!* The tempo of the horse, carousel, and music increases.

Overhead lights flash on and off, bedazzling everyone. It seems no time has passed, no events, no years separate Lucy from her childhood.

She is young again. She is there now, exhilarated, as her horse charges forward. Spiraling faster and faster, up and down, forward and over she goes, agelessly.

"Hang on tight, Lucy," she hears Mommy call from the sideline. Lucy clutches the column just in time. Horsey tosses his head, snorts, neighs, and gallops off into the mist, leaving the spinning carousel behind.

"It is so dark here. Where are we, Horsey?"

"Anywhere you want to be."

"Anywhere? Any place? Any time?"

"You may have three wishes to go anywhere you want to go."

"Three wishes? Are you a genie?"

"No, just a magic horsey."

"OOOOO! a magic horsey with three wishes for me."

"Where shall it be?"

"Take me to a place where I can buy a princess gown."

"Beverly Hills?"

"Yeah!"

"Next stop Saks Fifth Avenue."

"Whoopee!"

"We are here. I will pick you up in an hour."

"Perfect."

"May I help you miss?" asks the Gown Specialist.

"Yes, I need a gown with lace, real diamonds, and pearls."

"Ok, I have just the thing."

The Gown Specialist returns with a pink glittering taffeta and chiffon gown that has a heart of diamonds on the bodice and strands of pearls on the skirt.

"Oh, it's perfect. May I try it on?"

"No need to change. You are wearing it now."

Lucy looks down and then in the mirror. She is a princess right out of a fairy tale.

"Look at me!"

"You are lovely. Shall I call your horse?

"Yes, please."

"Look Horsey! I am a real princess."

"Exquisite. Where to now?"

"I am a princess. I must have a palace. Take me there."

"Next stop: Princess Lucy's Palace."

"Oh; it's beautiful! I love the gardens. I want to go inside and see what it's like."

"Ok, I'll be back after a while to see if you still have a third wish."

"Later, Horsey."

When Lucy enters the palace, she hears an argument between palace dignitaries. In the drawing room, Baron I, a short, stocky man in purple breeches and a brocade waistcoat declares, "It is time for a war. To balance our budget we must wage a war on a neighboring country."

Baron II, a tall gangly gentleman in dark habit with a red silk kerchief around his neck, studded buckled shoes with red-painted heels, and a cane hanging from his waistcoat button retorts, "No, no, wars are costly. We will simply raise the rent of the tenant farmers."

"That may cause a civil war."

"Nonsense, I won't hear of it. No wars, I say. It is all about power; we must show them who is boss."

"But…."

They are both red in the face and shaking their fists at each other by the time Lucy bursts into the room. She cannot stand this conversation about power and killing people. "We are not going to kill anyone or raise rents for any reason."

"Oh, it's that princess interfering again. I thought she was locked up in the garret. How did she get out?" asks Baron I.

"I was locked up? Why?"

"You babble. You never know what you're talking about." answers Baron II.

"You have your nerve. I don't think you know what *you're* talking about."

"YOU ARE MAD!"

"Says who?"

"Guards! Call the Royal Physician and let him know that the Mad Princess has broken out again."

"Wait! You can't do this to me!" Lucy yells for her life, as the guards drag her up to the garret. "Horsey, Horsey, where are you Horsey? I need that third wish."

"There she goes again, rattling on about some imaginary horse. Lock her up quickly."

Confined, she calls out again, "Horsey, Horsey, where are you? I am locked up."

Horsey appears inside the garret door, with a sneer and a snort, "Here I am Lucy. What goes?"

"This Palace is a terrible place. I am very sad here. All they talk about is money and war. And they make fun of me and do not give me the respect I deserve."

"It's good you still have one wish left. Make it a good one. Select a lasting one that will give you peace and keep you safe."

"Yes, yes, I will! Let's see. When and where did I last feel peaceful and safe?"

"Got it yet?"

"Yes! Back at the retirement community, lying on the chaise lounge by the saline pool."

"Oh, sounds like you know what your last wish is."

"Yes. Please take me HOME."

"We're on our way…we're almost there."

"There's the pool. I'm home."

"Till we meet again, Lucy."

"Thank you, Horsey. It's been the ride of a lifetime."

"Good to see you back, Lucy. How was your trip?" Rita asked.

"Wonder-filled, dear friend."

Card on the Loose

Joe prided himself in paying his bills on time. He had no debts. He checked his online bank account every day, making sure he had a consistent record of debits. He was also conscientious about his health. "Biological age of 55," said his doctor. He could still touch his toes at his current age of 70. For as long as he could remember, he had been all about staying active; a basketball star in college, a swimmer, a weight lifter, and until recently a jogger. He was an organized person with a positive outlook on life.

There was one thing, however, that he didn't seem to have any control over— his insomnia. He'd tried natural remedies like Melatonin, Valerian, and chamomile tea which didn't help. He frequently didn't fall asleep until 2:00 a.m., and sometimes not at all. Maybe he had restless leg syndrome as his doctor said, but he wasn't about to experience the side effects of any medicine his doctor wanted to prescribe. "It's just because I haven't had much exercise lately. That's why I can't sleep," he'd told the doctor. He'd slowed down a bit in his senior years, only because of a torn meniscus in his knee, which made running painful. Refusing pain medication, he was all for it when the doctor suggested physical therapy. *After the therapy, I'll pick up where I left off. I don't need any sleep or pain pills. Those things make you unsteady. Every day someone is falling and breaking something when they are on those. Not for me, no way!*

Physical therapy made him feel even more energetic at night. To make himself tired enough to sleep, he shuffled paperwork, watched TV, read, and walked or stomped numerous times around his living room. Usually, that worked. But one night, it didn't. After paying his utilities, watching the Late Show, reading twenty pages in his current novel, and completing 10 rounds in the living room, he turned on his computer one last time, just to check on the posting of a deposit that he'd made earlier that day. Bleary-eyed, but meticulous, he typed in his username and password to open his online bank statement. "What's this?" The deposit made that afternoon was "processing" along with an unfamiliar debit... for $984.24... to a mobile phone company.

"What the hell is this?" he yelled in the direction of his dog, Hector, who was sleeping peacefully. Startled, Hector woke up barking. To his shaggy best friend, he shouted, "I don't have that! I have a Tracfone!"

"Auuag," Hector whined.

"I never signed up for any dumb mobile service! The Tracfone only cost me $10. Somebody's gotten hold of my debit card. But, how could they? It's in my wallet! See! It's in my wallet! I *always* keep it there." Joe displayed the card to Hector.

Hector grumbled and barked some more, got up and walked over to Joe and sniffed his pocket for treats, and then laid his head on Joe's knee.

Joe stared at the screen. He couldn't believe his eyes. Hoping it had been all in his imagination, he waited for the figures to fade, but they sure didn't. The $984.24 just glared back at him. His heart began to beat rapidly. He took some slow deep breaths to calm himself down and fend off a possible heart attack. *Obviously, this is a fraudulent entry. I'll just call the bank and take care of it.*

Hector wandered back to his bed. Believing everything was peaceful again, the faithful companion closed his eyes and went back to sleep, while Joe's hazy orbs snapped into high focus as he searched the screen for and located the bank's phone number on the website.

A recording answered, "Thank you for calling the bank." You have reached the Customer Service Department. Our hours are from 9:00 AM to 7:00 PM. Please call back during the hours of service." Joe looked at the bottom of the screen. It was 1:00 AM, an inopportune time to discover a case of a counterfeit charge that threatened his meager assets.

He scanned the bank's website again and found a link called "Make a Claim." *At least I can put something in writing tonight.* He sighed when he stumbled across the statement, "You must wait until a debit is done processing before making a claim."

Shouting out loud again, he woke Hector a second time. "Someone has access to my bank account, and I can't do a thing about it… till it is… it is 'done processing.' Isn't that the pits? That stinks! That is the last thing I want it to do… process, my eye!" Joe complained to Hector, whose lids had just about closed. With a single growl, the dog turned towards the wall and went back to sleep. Joe looked at him, furiously. "Whoever said 'a dog had a hard life'? Don't blame me, if your treats disappear. Hope you like leftovers."

Sleep for me? Out of the question! I'll not sleep until this thing is resolved. Guess I'll do some more exercises. Maybe, they will knock me out.

"1-2-3-4…," Joe chanted as he resumed his treks around the living room, lifted weights, and pulled on stretch bands. Finally, after a half hour of yoga, he dosed off and awoke before sunrise.

The next morning, after swallowing a stiff cup of coffee, he wondered, *Who should I call first? Identity Theft? The Bank? the Psycho Ward? What did I do to deserve this? Is this some kind of card karma? Haven't I lived a clean life? My card was always in my possession. How in the world did someone get access to my account???*

He tried calling customer service at the bank first. "Thank you for calling the bank. Your call is important to us. Customer Service Representatives are currently helping other customers. You are 10th in line. Your wait time is approximately 20 minutes."

"What? 20 minutes?" But he waited; he had no choice. He flipped on his computer, and sure enough, the $984.24 charge was still there. "Damn! No one has caught the mistake yet! Somebody is getting away with murder!"

"Thank you for waiting. How may I help you today?"

"Someone has used my debit card to buy a mobile service, and all I have is a simple Tracfone that cost $10 with pay-as-you-go."

"May I have your name and account number?"

"Yes, yes, one minute. I will get my card." Perturbed, Joe complains, mindlessly. "How could someone get away with this? I always keep my card in my wallet, and I always pay my bills on time."

"Yes sir. Please tell me your name and card number, so I can look up your account."

"Sure, sure. Joe Weston, account number 3462-7742-3390."

"OK, Mr. Weston. Give me a moment while I access your information."

Hector was yawning and stretching and walking to the back door to be let out. Joe, holding the phone, got up and opened the door for him.

"Yes, Mr. Weston, I have your account up on my computer now. What figure are you disputing?"

Joe made his way back to the computer, knocking his coffee over. "One minute please. I have to wipe up my coffee."

"Your what?"

"My coffee. I spilled my coffee."

"What figure are you disputing, Mr. Weston?"

"The nine hundred eighty four dollars and twenty four cents entry."

"I see. Well, that hasn't finished processing yet. You can't dispute it or make a claim until it's cleared."

"But I don't want it to clear."

"Have you tried calling the mobile company?"

"But, it's the weekend! Somebody could be going on a shopping spree with my card!"

"You can file claims on whatever has posted."

"Oh, great!"

"I would advise you to check your credit report and call the mobile company."

"Sure, sure. Ok, Ok. I will."

"Is there anything else that I can assist you with today, Mr. Weston?"

"Nope. Nothing."

"Have a great day."

"Yeah, sure."

"Thank you for calling the bank. You will receive a survey to fill out in your email."

"Right. I can't wait."

The Customer Service person was silent.

"Right. Sure, great, thanks. Goodbye."

"Good bye, Mr. Weston."

"Woof. Woof." Hector was scratching at the back door. Joe let him in. "They said I need to call the mobile company, and check my credit report." Hector walked towards his food bowl and gave it a shove. "Okay, Okay." Joe filled his bowl with kibble and dropped back into his desk chair, exhausted and disgusted. "Life is supposed to be easy when you get old!" Hector was busy munching his food and didn't look up, even when Joe continued to stare at him. Joe's stomach began to grumble; but, he was determined to get to the bottom of the matter at hand before breakfast.

Just then he noticed an 800 telephone number on the electronic bank statement for the said mobile phone service. *I'll give it a shot.* By now, Hector was ready for a new day and was scratching at the door to be let out again. He was full of pep, unlike Joe who had essentially spent the night standing up.

After opening the door for Hector, Joe dialed the number of the mobile service. It was answered by a robot, which asked him to enter the phone number associated with his service. Of course, he couldn't do that, since he didn't have service with the company in the first place. He had no choice but to let the automaton have its say. Finally, having received no response from the caller, the robot transferred Joe to a real person, who asked, "May I have the phone number associated with your account?"

"I don't have an account with your company."

"Calling to set up an account? What is your first and last name?

"No, no. I don't want to set up an account."

"Then why are you calling? How may I help you, Sir?"

"Someone used *my* debit card number to pay *you* for *their* phone from *your* company! Maybe *they* even put it in *my* name."

"What is your name?"

"Joseph Weston."

"I'll check my records.... No, I don't have your name on any account."

"Don't you check to make sure the name matches the card number?"

"Well, who knows when somebody gives somebody the right to use their card? People do it with their kids all the time. We have no way of knowing that."

"That is ridiculous!"

"I truly regret you are having this problem, Mr. Weston. But we really can't help you if you don't have the service phone number or the name of the client. Have you tried calling your bank?"

"Yes, of course. Good bye. Thanks for your help." Joe slammed down the phone.

Okay, next. I have ID protection. I'll check my credit report. I'll get to the bottom of this, hopefully before I explode. Joe staggered into the bathroom and put his head under the sink faucet to cool off and keep himself going. Then, he sat down and took a few long deep breaths, again.

"Woof, woof!" Hector was at the back door scratching. Joe opened the door to see Hector wagging his tail with a tennis ball in his mouth, which he dropped at Joe's feet. Joe tossed the ball into the yard. "I'll catch you later, buddy." He was sorry to disappoint Hector, but he had to take care of business before it would be too late. *The guy could be buying a new car with my card right now!*

Back at the computer, he entered his username and password for the insurance company where he had an ID protection policy. But there was a second level of protection that required another username and password to get into the actual credit report. Did he have that password? No! So, he hit the "forgot your password?" link and answered the requested questions. He knew where he was born and what his birthdate was, so he dutifully put in the information. But, the computer had the nerve to say his answers were incorrect. So, he called the insurance company for help. And *its robot* said, "Please call the credit reporting company Monday thru Friday, during regular business hours."

For the remainder of the weekend, Joe overloaded on chips, beer, and football. Then bright and early on Monday morning, he called the insurance company.

"Hello, my name is Joe Weston and someone has made fraudulent use of my debit card to buy a mobile phone service. The last time that I used my debit card was in the gas station."

"Oh, this is a common complaint. From now on, pay inside the gas station. Someone must have pulled your information off of the pump after you left. It happens a lot," said the insurance company.

"Oh, I can't believe it! Isn't anything sacred anymore?"

"May I help you with anything else, sir?"

"No, no, no. You've done enough."

"Thank you for calling. Have a nice day."

"Right and I don't do surveys."

Joe checked is bank statement and discovered that the $984 and twenty four cents was still "processing."

That does it! It was time for drastic measures! *I will put an end to this sapping of my time, money, and energy…and sanity!* He called the bank and cancelled his debit card.

The bank clerk actually offered some information of use this time. "You will need to go to your local bank and get a temporary card since you will not receive the new card for 7-10 business days." So, Joe set aside his priorities for Monday, including his daily workout at the gym, drove to the bank, and marched in. He was given a temporary card by a bank officer who actually called some central office and got the fraudulent nine hundred eighty-four dollars and twenty-four cents backed out of his account. Now he planned to go home and get started on everything he needed to get done that day before he had been so sidetracked. When he arrived, he promptly fell asleep on the couch.

Later that day, after the bank was closed, he checked his online account just to be sure, and the $984.24 had been subtracted from his balance. *All right!*

He finally got into his credit report and it reflected nothing fraudulent, which made him happy that no one had further compromised his account. That is, he was happy until he went to buy gas several days later and the temporary card didn't work. Fortunately, deep in his wallet he had a somewhat crumbled check which had not seen the daylight for months. He was able to use the check to buy gas.

When he called the bank, he was told, "The number on the temporary card has expired. We will be sending you a permanent card in 7-10 business days."

So, in the bank, he wrote a check to himself for enough cash to get him through 7-10 business days, believing that when he received his new credit card in the mail this nightmare would be over. The only problem was that when he called the bank to register the new card, the robot on the phone rejected it. *Why do they have stupid robots handling these important matters? Robots aren't saving me any time!*

So he took another trip to the bank to report the new error and to get cash to last him another 7-10 days. Once again, the bank promised to send him yet another new debit card. It looked promising, until a merchant tried to scan the latest debit card and he had to go home without the purchase because the bank didn't recognize the card.

Maybe it's time to switch banks. No, the last bank mishandled a deposit that screwed up a car purchase. Life is just what it is, I suppose. I guess one can't control everything in life.

In the backyard, Joe tossed the ball for Hector. Happy to have his pal back, Hector joyfully chased and recovered the ball. Joe gave him a treat and Hector wagged his tail. Things were back to normal.

After that, life got better for no particular reason. Even though Joe wasn't able to jog again after physical therapy, he did increase his swimming and indoor bike time and he slept when he was tired, whatever time that occurred. And the next card remained stable for about a year.

About the Author

Arlene Cohen has lived a life punctuated by acute moments of disbelief that have inspired her to make sense of them through the written word. She has taught Creative Movement and performed Dancing Stories in schools, libraries, and community centers. She has received grants from the National Endowment for the Arts and Humanities, the Hawaii Culture and Arts Foundation, and the Regional Arts and Culture Council in Portland, Oregon. She received an MLS in Children's Librarianship from the University of Hawaii where she was an Academic Librarian, and Storytelling Instructor in the Speech Department.

Website: literacyonthemove.com
Email: BeAtPeace2003@yahoo.com

www.ingramcontent.com/pod-product-compliance
Lightning Source LLC
Chambersburg PA
CBHW071009120726
47910CB00004B/1450